SETTLING

TOY

Copyright © 2020 by Toy

All rights reserved.

No part of this book may be reproduced in any form or by any electronic or mechanical means, including information storage and retrieval systems, without written permission from the author, except for the use of brief quotations in a book review.

CHAPTER 1

abril

Sitting down here in my man cave bored as hell but, this was the only place I could have peace of mind. It's a damn shame that my home life had become nothing more than a pile of excuses not to be up under the woman I chose to be with. That's the funny thing about the word chose. On the surface it means that you made a choice but, in my case the choice was being made for me. I would rather be up under my baby mama and my baby girl but, shit was complicated with us. It wasn't like we didn't get along because we did but, I just understood the fact that me knocking on her door to tell her that with my family is where I wanted to be wasn't in the cards or the future right now.

Things with Ciana and I weren't past the point of not being fixed but, honestly they weren't broken in the first place. Ciana and our daughter Iyanna had my heart, I would do anything for them to be happy. Right now, that includes letting her relationship run its course with that nigga Akeem. I was just playing the role and bidding my time. He was bound to fuck up because that's what niggas did. He hated the fact that I was extremely active in my daughter's life. Iyanna's little slick ass would always want to do shit with me and her mother. I laughed every time she would hit me with the 'can mommy hang with us' line. I knew what she was doing that's why I never called her little sneaky ass out on it. I would ask her all the time if that nigga had done anything to her or her mother. Every time she would say no. I was cordial to him just like Ciana was cordial to my girl Porsche. Just thinking about those two together in the same space was enough to make a simp nigga crazy. I was not one of those niggas that got involved in whatever bullshit ass argument they would have. Porsche knew not to cross the line and disrespect Ciana. Ciana on the other hand would use that mouth of hers to make you want to slap the taste out of it. I swear she would make Ghandi want to punch the shit out of her ass. Porsche would always fuss about how I had Ciana up on a pedestal which is a fact that I will never deny. I don't know why she always wanted to point the shit out. A few times I asked her if she was so damn pissed about how I moved why was she even with me in the first place. She would tell me because she loves me but, she was lying through her damn teeth. She may have had feelings for me but, love wasn't one of those feelings. She likes the fact that by being my girl put her on a level that her bird ass friends would never see. Porsche was bad as fuck to look at no bullshit looking ass bitch would ever be on my arm but, her mind was childish, lazy, petty and paranoid as hell. She had a body of an Instagram model. There wasn't a day she wasn't put together from head to toe. She stayed with those fake ass bundles that reached the small of her back. I still say she's had some work done to her body but, she swears everything about her is natural. I would call her ass out about it every time. How the fuck is everything about her natural but, she walks around with bundles, someone else's eyelashes, and the Chinese people's fingernails. Don't get me started on how she was walking around with the counterfeit version of every damn designer there was. You couldn't tell her ass shit though.

When I got with her she was just something to do to keep my mind off Ciana's hot and cold ass. I regret getting with her. I know that's fucked up to say but, it was the truth. I started bringing Porsche around hoping that would make Ciana come to her senses but, she fooled the fuck out of me. Instead of her realizing that we need to make us work she went and found Akeem's ass. When she first brought the nigga around I told her ass I didn't like him. I knew that wasn't gonna change shit but, I wanted to let her know. I can hear what her smart ass said clear as day 'I'll put your complaint in the complaint divisions file. They'll address it when they get a chance'. That was the shit she would say to me. I think she low-key wanted me to choke the shit out of her ass.

"Are you staying down here all night?" Porsche came in asking me.

"If I do would it be a problem?" I asked.

"I hate it when you answer my questions with questions. I want us to go out get some drinks or something. We haven't been out in a while," she told me.

I rolled my eyes because she was out of her fucking mind if she thought I believed that shit. Her wanting us to go out only meant that she had a place in mind because one of her bird ass friends were going out and she wanted to have the spotlight on her instead of them. Porsche was just what I needed to keep me from being out here being reckless fucking randoms. If you think about it her ass was a constant random in my world. That shit was an oxymoron like a motherfucker. She had her own place but, lately she has been here with me more and more. I should just come out and tell her that she's tripping thinking that we need to be out just for her to show off. I wasn't in the mood to argue so I tried to avoid the conversation all together.

"Oh yeah," was my response.

She stood there looking at me like her staring at me moved me.

"I bet if your baby mama called wanting to go out you would go," she fussed. That right there is another reason why she would never be more than she was to me right now. I shook my head because I damn sure didn't want to go through this shit with her today. She was gonna mess around and get her plastic ass feelings hurt. "I know you hear me Jabril," she continued.

"Man come on with all that shit. If you wanna go out to show up ya so-called friends leave me out of the shit. When you get in front of them the way you act ain't cool. If you wanna go out be my guest. Leave me out of the shit," I told her.

"If we're going to be together we're gonna be around my friends. You need to get used to being around them. It will make our relationship go smoother," she said seriously.

"Aye, I already said all I'm gonna say. If you want to go out with the bird gang then do you. I ain't going," I told her.

"How are you gonna call my girls some birds?"

"I always call them birds because that's exactly what they are. Porsche just go ahead and do whatever you're gonna do. I got a ton of shit on my mind right now. You doing all that talking is making my blunt that I just smoked fade out. Move around with all that," I told her.

"I don't even know why I deal with this shit sometimes," she said kissing her teeth. I don't understand why she wanted to push my ass tonight. If she wanted to skate I wasn't holding her ass hostage.

"I don't think you want me to go down that road with you right now,"

"Don't act like you don't know it's the truth. I'm not an ugly bitch so I can go out here and get me a nigga that's gonna cherish me," she said not understanding that she was about to be crying. I wasn't in the mood for this right now. I tried to warn her.

"Go find his ass then. I'm not making you stick around shawty. If you don't want to be here why the fuck ain't ya feet moving? You know that attitude you're throwing isn't gonna move me. Take your ass on before I turn the heat up in this bitch and melt your ass where you stand," I told her.

"Melt me? Wow how disrespectful can you be. I see why your baby mama don't wanna be with you. I keep telling you I didn't have any work done to my body," she said sounding like I hurt her feelings.

"Tell the truth the only thing you haven't had work on is the inside of your pussy and the soles of your feet. I still say you may have had that pussy tightened up though. Stop bringing up my baby mama too. I don't know why you always bringing her up but, stop that shit. Insecurity ain't cute in any way, shape, or form,"

"Fuck you, Jabril!"

"Shit I would rather you come in here trying to fuck me instead of fuck with me but, aye we all make choices," I said with a shrug.

"How can you talk about me and talk about fucking me at the same time?"

"I do it easy just like you got all that damn work done then forgot about the shit. P take your ass out and find a nigga that likes collecting barbie dolls cuz, I'm not him," I told her.

"You make me sick!"

"That's coming from a person that is still here in my face. Stay, or go whichever one you chose will be good with me just get the fuck out my face," I told her.

She did her little dramatic spin move and stomped out of the man cave giving me the peace and quiet that I needed. I don't know how long I can keep this shit going with her. Tomorrow she'll be over here like nothing happened.

CHAPTER 2

iana

Checking myself out in the mirror I had to smile at the baddie that I saw looking back at me. Having Iyanna helped me get to where I was right now physically. I loved my baby, but it's hard for me to look at her sometimes when I think about how I was going to abort her when I first found out I was pregnant. I'm grateful to the man above and my big head baby daddy for showing me that having her was the way to go. She brightened my days just by looking at me with all the hope in her eyes. She was a mess though with her slick mouth and attitude. I know she has it from both sides so she can't fight it. However, when she gets a little beyond herself I have no problem getting her ass back in line. Thankfully she was over my best friend Bali's house for the next two nights. Tonight, I was going to show my man some appreciation. I had everything set but, knowing Akeem we would be fucking about ten minutes after he comes through the door.

I'm so happy that I met him. He helped me realize that you shouldn't have to wait for someone to show you how special you are they should show you every day. When I met Akeem Shafir, I was in a bad way. My baby daddy was plucking my nerves on purpose and not letting me do me but, while still doing him. It was a few weeks after he started bringing his bitch around. No, I don't call her a bitch because I want to get with him or because we're not together. I call her a bitch because that's exactly what she is. I still say something is off about her although I don't have proof but, I can feel it in my bones that her ass is on some bullshit. Sooner or later everything will come out though I'm sure of that. Anyway, Jabril and I were still fucking around on the low then he pops up with this bitch. I know he expected me to act a fool but, instead I kept it moving and happened to meet Akeem's tall, dark, sexy ass. This man was enough to make my mouth water when we met and he had on his work uniform. He worked as an HVAC - tech. His uniform had a few dirt spots on it and was looking so damn manly on him at that moment. I gave him my number and we've been chilling ever since. Bali thinks that although Akeem is sexy he's just a place holder until Jabril and I get our lives together. I keep trying to tell her that Jabril is not thinking about me in that way. He has his bitch and I have Akeem. Sometimes life doesn't work out to be a fairytale for everyone. I wasn't gonna dwell on a damn thing.

"Baby, where are you?" Akeem yelled.

I wasn't expecting him so early. I thought I had at least another two hours before he came home. Most of the food was done but, the main dish was still in the oven. I went into the living room where I found him and one of his creepy ass friends. I didn't know many of his friends because I'm not the type of girlfriend that has to be seen by all the niggas. I usually try to separate myself from them when he brings them around. There were only a few that I even spoke to and this guy staring at me right now is not one of the ones I speak to. He didn't bring him around much but, when he did I hated the way he stared at me.

"Oh shit, you could've told me you were bringing someone

with you," I fussed then made a sharp turn to head back into the room.

"Damn," I heard the guy say.

I was in the room putting on a jogging suit when my room door opened.

"Bae my bad about bringing Carlos with me, I apologize for not telling you. I wasn't expecting you to be in come fuck me mode," he said laughing.

I don't know what the hell he thought was so damn funny.

"Why didn't you take him to your place? What the hell is he here for anyway?" I asked.

"I came to see about you before I go out of town for the next four days," he said nonchalantly.

"Out of town? You didn't say anything about going out of town yesterday, last night, or this morning. When did you find all this out?" I asked.

He looked around, took a deep breath, and pulled on his beard a few times. All those actions are ones that scream to me that he's lying his ass off. This isn't the first time I've suspected him of being a damn fraud with his words. I just didn't have the proof that he was lying or even doing something underhanded. I was sure to side eye him.

"I just found out a little bit ago. Carlos and I have a job to handle in Connecticut. From what they told us it will take anywhere from four days to two weeks to get done," he said.

"You just told me four days but, now you saying it could take up to two weeks. What the hell is going on with you? It's not like you work for the government or anything so what's up with the emergency and the secrecy? Don't sit there and tell me there's an HVAC emergency that none of the HVAC people in Connecticut can't handle. If I find out you're lying you might as well stay with whatever bitch that you're going to go see. I ain't for the bullshit, Akeem," I told him.

"There you go. I keep telling you that I'm not trying to do no slick shit. This is a job thing. There ain't shit I can do about it. You think I don't want to be up under you instead of crawling in a hole somewhere? Come on Bae don't act like that. Where's babygirl?" He asked.

I know he's trying to change the subject but, I wasn't with it tonight.

"She's at Bali and Ish's house for the weekend. You should get going being that you have to pack," I told him as I walked past him.

"Don't act like that Bae. I told you it's for work," he pleaded as he walked behind me.

"You knew how I was gonna act when you came in here with that bullshit in mind. Don't think because you brought homie in here that I was gonna curb what I was going to say to you about this bullshit mystery assignment. Go head go do you and whatever HVAC emergency there is that you want me to believe," I responded not paying his ass no mind. I did hear his little buddy snicker at what I was saying. He knew what Akeem was saying was a damn lie just like I did. I just couldn't prove it right now. His time was coming though. Trust and believe all his bullshit was going to catch up to his ass.

"Man, I don't want to leave with you being mad and shit,"

"I'm not mad but, I'm not stupid either, Akeem," I said rolling my eyes.

"I'll call you when I get settled at the hotel," he said.

"Sure Bob," I told him still not looking in his direction. He went back down the hallway. I could feel his little friend staring at me. I know that Akeem wasn't in the room with us but, damn he was bold as hell with his eyeballs.

"You deserve more," he told me.

I looked up to ask him what the hell that meant but, Akeem came back into the living room saying that he was ready to go. They walked out leaving me stuck wondering what the hell did Akeem really have going on?

Akeem had only been full of shit like this for the past couple of months. I know that we were still a new couple in my eyes but, there was something else that was off with him. When we got together it was all roses, bubble baths and romantic nights. After six months of being together the long nights, few compliments, attitude, and lies started. It was as if as soon as he got comfortable he switched up. I was hoping his ass would switch back but, it hasn't happened yet. I know I was gonna have to break up with him whenever he got back from this supposedly work trip. I knew in my gut it wasn't a work trip if there was a trip at all. A part of me wanted to follow him and see what the hell he's really up to but, the other part of me didn't care that much to put in the extra effort. My phone going off made me get up and push the thoughts of Akeem's shifty behavior to the back of my mind.

"Yeah," I answered.

"Your ass better be getting dressed," Bali asked me.

"Getting dressed? Dressed for what?" I asked.

"We're going out tonight. Ish has the kids so get dressed," she said not letting me get a word in to tell her ass yes or no.

I had to laugh because that's the move I usually pull on her. I don't have shit to lose so I got my happy ass up and got dressed. A night out with my girl could be just what I need.

Akeem

"Why the hell you in there eyeballing Ciana and shit?" I asked Carlos.

"Man, this whole situation is about to blow up in y'all face. The shit is stupid and you need to stop before you go too far," he said.

I don't know what the deal is with Carlos lately. His ass has been on some righteous shit. That's the type of shit that I don't need. There isn't a righteous bone in my body. Carlos and I met while I was locked up on some bullshit domestic violence charge. Up until now I never had to question his loyalty. I heard what he told Ciana but, I don't get the point of him telling her that shit in the first place. It was already too much with him starring at her and shit.

"We got this so don't be concerned about shit but what you're supposed to do. If you do something to fuck this up I won't hesitate to kill your ass," I told him.

He could sit over there acting like he wasn't a part of this but he damn well was. He needed to go to confessional or go pray to whatever god he recognized this month and leave it the fuck alone. Jabril was going to pay for what he did and that was that. Nothing or no-one was stopping his life from ending just like he helped with the ending of my brother and cousin lives.

"Does he even know who you are? I know y'all have been around each other with you fucking his baby mom and shit. He hasn't once paid you any mind?" Carlos asked.

"If he knows who I am then he hasn't said shit to me about it. That nigga's got the enemy right up in his circle and he's too fucked up to even notice. I did hear that he was trying to get out of the street shit that he's been doing. We're gonna have to get at his ass before that happens. The last thing I need is for him to get out then I won't have an opportunity to get at him without looking suspect," I told him.

I knew what the fuck I had going on. Carlos was too wishy washy to know all the details of what was gonna go down. I just need him to be the face of the contact person. I couldn't do it because he knows my ass and my partner damn sure couldn't do it without raising suspicions. Carlos didn't know who I had working with me but, he knew I wasn't doing this alone. We pulled up to the hotel that we would be staying at for the next few days. I had been laying low trying to piece together a plan and now it was time to put my shit in motion. I owed it to my family to avenge the deaths of my brother and cousin. Jabril was damn sure gonna pay.

CHAPTER 3

*J*abril

I was walking into my brother's house to chop it up with him about some shit that's been on my mind. I knew that my baby-girl was over here so I could see her for a few as well. Chilling with my people was always the best form of relaxation for me. I was in a good mood because Porsche didn't bother coming to my house last night after she went out with the bird gang. I was relieved that she was wherever she was instead of her coming to my house picking a fucking argument. I sometimes wondered if being single would be better for me. That thought would leave when I thought about how more pussy brought about more problems. It didn't matter if you made the chic sign a contract saying no feelings just fucking would be involved, I can guarantee that her ass was gonna catch fucking feelings. Then came the questions, the bullshit ass tears, the accusations and all the other bullshit would come.

"Where you at Ish?" I called out as I opened the door.

"Daddy, daddy, daddy," my babygirl came running to me with her arms wide open and some type of food covering her face.

"Whoa, whoa what is all over your face?" I asked as I jogged in the other direction. Me trying to get away from her only made her stop running and laugh harder. That little girl was as silly as they come. Her little laugh was all I needed to hear to put my mood in a better place.

"It's ice cream daddy!" She screamed.

"Ish! Come help me man. Iyanna is in here trying to get me dirty with her ice cream face," I called out.

We were still running around the sofa. She thought this was a game but, I was dead ass. I couldn't walk around the rest of the day with her ice cream all over my clothes.

"Iyanna come here child. You know how your daddy is about getting his clothes dirty," Ciana said.

I wasn't expecting her to be here too. Why the hell was she here and not at home? I stopped jogging when I heard her voice and that's when Iyanna ran smack dab into my leg. Yep, that damn ice cream was all over my damn jeans.

"Ah man you got my pants dirty," I said as I picked Iyanna up tossing her in the air a couple of times. She was laughing so loud that I knew it would only be a matter of time before everybody comes to find out what was happening to her. I put her back down on the floor then watched her take off running again.

"What you doing over here so early? Is everything good with you and Kahbib?" I asked Ciana.

She stood there looking at me like I was crazy. Yes, I know her man's name but, he didn't matter just like his name didn't. She knew what it was because she did the same thing with Porsche.

"Everything is good. Bali and I went out last night. I came here instead of going home to an empty bed," she answered.

"Empty?" I asked.

"Yes, empty he went out of town on some emergency job," she said while rolling her eyes.

I didn't want to laugh in her face but, I did. There ain't no way his job, if he had one, was sending his ass anywhere. She cut her eyes at me so I kept my thoughts to myself for now. I was gonna have to check his ass out though. If he was lying to her about where he was then something was up with him. I had promised her that I wasn't gonna check out any more of her boyfriends but, this was gonna be the exception.

"Oh okay," was all I said.

"That's all you have to say?" She asked.

I know she was expecting an argument but, I couldn't argue with her without proof. So, until I had that I was gonna be the bigger person.

"Yeah, what else am I supposed to say. He's yo nigga if you think he cool going out of town for an emergency job even though he ain't a cop, Ems, nurse, doctor, teacher, electrician, pastor, or even a damn basketball coach then hey who am I to say you're being stupid for this nigga," I told her.

She rolled her eyes and kissed her teeth just like she always does. I wasn't gonna sit there and go back and forth with her so I left her standing there looking as stupid as she was being right now. I went to find my brother in his office. He was going over some paperwork that had him so wrapped up that he didn't look up when I walked in. So, me being the brother that I am I slammed the door shut making his ass look up.

"What the fuck is wrong with you? What you here for this early anyway? Hold up you and Ciana ain't back fucking with each other are y'all? I know she came in last night with Bali and then your ass is here. Don't be fucking in my house man," Ish told me with a serious look on his face.

"I just got here not too long ago. I didn't know Ciana was

gonna be here. No, we ain't fucking and no we ain't fucking in your house," I said shaking my head.

"So, what's up? You're usually out handling business this time of morning," he said sitting back in his big ass office chair.

"I'm about to wrap up my dealings in the street," I told him.

Ish and I had an unspoken rule after he went all the way legitimate. I didn't discuss anything street related with him. He knew I was in the streets but, he had no specifics on what I was out here doing. Since Iyanna's been born I've been thinking about making some changes. The first major change will be me getting out of the streets completely.

"Are you in a position to do that?" He asked.

"Yeah I am. You know me I move to the beat of my own drum. I deal with what and who I want to deal with. I don't owe no damn body and so I can just stop when I get ready,"

"You're sure you're ready now?" He asked.

"Yeah,"

"I'm just asking because I know how impulsive you can be. You're addicted to the adrenaline rush you get from completing a deal with no problems. I'm not gonna lie sometimes I miss it but, I made the right choice. What do you need me to do?" He asked.

"I need you to be here to make sure I'm done with all things street in the next four months," I told him.

"What about your girl? Have you told her yet? You know that she's one of those types that gets off on her man being a street nigga. You getting out is gonna cause problems," he told me.

"I get what you're saying but, I look at it like this, if she wants me to keep putting my life and freedom on the line just to say she's with a street nigga then her ass ain't for me."

He wasn't telling me anything that I didn't know already.

Porsche isn't hiding the fact that she's who she is. I think that's why I keep her ass around. I know her motives.

"I'm with you on that. What else is on your mind?"

"I keep thinking that somethings are off in the atmosphere but, I can't put my finger on what it is exactly. I also need you to call your guy and do a background check on that Akeem nigga that Ciana's with," I said.

"I thought y'all weren't doing that shit anymore?" He asked.

He knew the story of the nigga that Ciana called herself fucking with before this Akeem nigga fell out of the sky. The nigga was a fucking con artist. He had a wrap sheet as long as a fucking Winnebago. The day I got the report I just so happened to run into the nigga. I beat the shit out of him and told him to stay the fuck away from Ciana and my daughter. It took Ciana almost three months to find out why dude had ghosted her ass. She was pissed with me for a while but, she got over it. We talked it out and she asked me to let her make her own mistakes. In any other situation I would be fine with that but, this nigga Akeem needs to be checked out. Somethings not right with his ass and I know it.

"Yeah well, if it comes back straight then she won't have to know," I said with a shoulder shrug.

"When are you gonna tell that woman that you love her?"

"Who said anything about love? She's the mother of my child. I have feelings for her and will always look out for her wellbeing. If she's good then Iyanna's good, it's my job to look out," I told him.

"Looking out, is that what you call this?"

"Call what? We both know we're not going down the relationship road. There ain't no need to even bring that shit up. I'm just looking out for both of them period. There ain't no other reason for anything that I do when it comes to Ciana," I told him. He shook his head at me and chuckled a little bit.

"What man? Everybody doesn't get to have the fairytale love that you and Bali have. Y'all shit is different and you know it," I told him.

"It's only different because I made the shit different. You and Ciana need to stop this bullshit that y'all are doing. It's only gonna end up with Porsche and Akeem getting hurt in the process because you two are too fucking stubborn to admit how y'all really feel. Life is too fucking short to be playing games," he told me.

"Ciana's ass is too fucking mean to check out of here before any of us," I told him.

It was the truth she was mean as shit regardless if she did it on purpose or not. Before we ended up in bed together we avoided each other because it was bound to be an argument if we were in the same room too long. Either she would say something that made me say something to her or I would say something just to fuck with her. When I first met her, I thought that her mouth was too fucking smart. Now after her having my daughter I still feel that way but, I learned how she thinks about somethings. I know when she's just fucking around and when she's really pissed. I know how to handle her. She was the least of my worries. Truthfully I was more worried about what her so-called man was up to.

CHAPTER 4

keem

Today was the day that Carlos was going to contact Jabril and get the ball rolling. As long as he stuck to the script everything should go smoothly.

"If you try to give him a heads up then you're gonna end up dead right along with his ass. Don't play superhero and fuck this up for us," I told him.

"Look you can keep those bullshit threats to yourself. I know that you or ya partner can't do my part because he knows y'all so either tell me to get the fuck on or stop threatening my ass. If I say I'm gonna do something then it'll get done. Anything else beyond that leave me the fuck alone about it," he told me.

I had to shake my head at his ass. I don't know who the fuck he thought he was talking to but, it damn sure isn't me. I two pieced his ass right in the middle of the room we were standing in. He took a couple of steps back and held his jaw. I was waiting on him to come at me with some more hot shit.

"You got it for right now. Don't get too comfortable with this shit though," he told me.

"Punk ass, I'm not gonna keep telling you that I run the show not you motherfucker,"

He only glanced at me and nodded again. I could see it in his eyes that I was most likely gonna have to kill his ass eventually. I didn't have a problem with that even though we had a long history of friendship. Carlos has always been a thorough nigga but, the only thing that didn't work to my advantage was that the nigga had a conscious. He would love to preach about doing the right thing so the right karma comes back to you.

"What if things didn't go down like you think it did? What if Jabril wasn't the reason why your people got killed that night?" Carlos asked.

I knew this question was coming from him because that was just how he was made. The problem was that I ain't the one to be explaining shit to nobody.

"You can waste your time trying to figure that shit out. The point is that Parker and Ali went to pick up some guns from this nigga. They dead and he's not. The shit is simple if you stop trying to make it complicated," I told him.

The truth is I never liked Jabril from the first time my brother started telling me about him. It was fucked up how my brother spoke so highly of the man that took his life. That was the streets for you. The streets don't love no damn body. I don't care how much pull or respect you think you have there's always that one person looking to take you out. I missed the fuck out of my brother and it was time for Jabril to pay for the shit he has done. Fuck him and his big named brother. They both were gonna hurt. Ish was gonna hurt when he finds out that his brother is dead. Jabril is gonna surely see my face and know why I'm killing him before he dies.

"I still say you're doing too much right now at least find out why things went down the way they did. You gotta admit the shit doesn't sound right," he went on.

I was tired of going back and forth with him. No matter what he says the shit went down and my family lost two people while his bitch ass walked away. In due time he'll pay for what he did. It was a shame that I couldn't kill his ass twice.

"Make the fucking call and put it on speaker," I told him.

I watched as he pulled out his phone to make the call. Although he was hesitating he still made it and placed the phone on the table with the speaker loud as it could go.

"Who dis," Jabril answered.

"I heard you're the man that can help me get some tools that I may need," Carlos said.

"Who the fuck is this? I ain't a fucking carpenter what the fuck imma do with some damn tools. I guess you got the wrong info nigga," Jabril said.

"I got ya number form Ali before he passed. I guess he was wrong then huh," Carlos said.

I knew that saying my brother's name would get his damn attention. He paused for a few minutes which meant he was thinking.

"Oh yeah, Ali gave you my number?"

"Yeah, I've been out of town on some business. I never needed to contact you until now but, it ain't no thang. I won't hit ya line again," Carlos said.

"Yo, meet me at the WAWA on Military Highway in an hour,"

"How you gonna know who I am? Don't you wanna know what kind of car I'm gonna be in or some shit like that?"

"Nah, just be there," Jabril said then he ended the call.

"Good thinking throwing Ali's name in there. He wasn't gonna talk to you otherwise,"

"Yeah, I know,"

We got our things together and headed down to the car. If he was saying he didn't need to know what car or any information so he could recognize Carlos that meant he was gonna try to get there before Carlos did. That only means that we have to get there before he does. Jabril wasn't the quiet one but, that didn't mean the nigga wasn't smart. He was one of the smartest guys in the street according to my brother Ali. We were only about ten minutes away from the gas station so I drove around the parking lot a few times just to check out the scene. As usual there were cars everywhere.

"Yo, ain't that ya girl's car?" Carlos asked getting my attention.

Sure enough there was Ciana's Infiniti truck pulling into the parking lot. Now, an optimistic nigga would think that this was a big ass coincidence but, not me. Why the fuck was she here right now at this moment? The passenger door opened and out came Jabril and Iyanna. I watched him look around the parking lot like he was looking for someone before they walked in the store. I called Ciana just to see what the fuck was up.

"Hey," she answered sounding all cheery and shit not knowing that I'm looking at her right now.

"What's up? What you got going on today?"

"Nothing just running some errands right now after that I'm going home and relax the rest of the day. How you doing?" She asked.

"Oh yeah, well make sure you put some gas in the truck," I told her before ending the call.

We watched her look around. I guess she was looking for me. Ciana had two vehicles to choose from, how would I know which one she's driving. She had no business hanging with Jabril like she was right now. They look like they're out enjoying a fucking family day. I hope for her sake that I'm thinking a little too much about this situation with her and that nigga.

"She's looking for you?" Carlos said while laughing.

It was a good thing that the tint on this car was damn near illegal because it was so dark. She could look all she wanted to with the dark tint and how far we were parked from her she couldn't see either of us in the car looking dead at her bogus ass. I was pissed to the point that I wanted to yank her ass out of the truck. Every time she was with this nigga it fucked with me heavy. I know that I'm with her under false pretenses and shit but, her ass didn't know what I had going on behind her back.

"This whole thing is bogus as fuck. Why the fuck she out with his ass like this?" I said as I hit the dashboard of the car.

"Chill nigga, that is her kid's pops. You can't go off because they in the car together and they got the kid with them. Ciana ain't the type to be moving flawed out here. I'm sure she's got a reason to be with him,"

"On some real shit you making me look at you a little funny. You all uplifting and shit for everybody that's crossed my ass. Let me find out you out here flawed," I told him.

He stayed quiet but, called Jabril on the phone as we saw him and the kid come out of the store.

"Yeah," he answered.

"I'm about five minutes away,"

"Cool I'm here," Jabril answered then ended the call.

Ciana had the truck parked so that we were diagonal from where she was. They couldn't see us pull out unless they turned to the right. At the moment they were talking to the kid so we got out of the parking lot unspotted. I got out at the burger king close to the WAWA while he drove back over to meet Jabril. While I took a seat inside the restaurant Ciana texted that she missed me. I shook my head because she damn sure had a funny way of showing it.

I watched from the window of the Burger King as Jabril got out of the truck again and walked over to the car that Carlos was waiting in. The Burger King was next to the WAWA so I had a full view of the parking lot and gas pumps. That particular one was always busy but, I was focused on the car that Carlos was driving. I was hoping that his dumb ass stayed in the car with the windows rolled up. Just as that thought crossed my mind his stupid ass got out of the car to dap up Jabril. I prayed that she didn't see his ass.

CHAPTER 5

abril

"What the hell you keep looking around for?"

Since getting in the truck with Ciana she was looking around like someone was either watching her or out to get her. There was no reason for her to be acting like she got a batch of bad drugs right now.

"Nothing, it's just .. nothing. Where is this guy you're supposed to be meeting with? You ought to be ashamed of yourself doing this shit right now," she told me.

We were supposed to have family day today. Iyanna got the bright idea that since we were all at her Uncle Ish's house that we might as well hang out together. This little girl was pimping both of us today. When this guy called saying that he needed some tools. I didn't see why we couldn't stop up here so I could look the nigga in his eyes and then be out for the rest of the day. It wasn't like there were any transactions going down. I just wanted to see what vibe I got off dude.

"I'm just having a conversation with dude that's it. It ain't gonna take that long so stop bitching,"

"Ohhh daddy you said bitch. Mama told me never let anyone call me a bitch. That's not nice," she told me.

I shook my head because I thought we passed the terrible twos the year before last but, I guess she's the word police now. Every time I turned around she was going in about something I said.

"I know baby. I'm sorry Ciana. Everything's gonna be good though,"

"I hope so. I thought you were done with all this?"

"Not yet but, I will be real soon. Nothing I told you before has changed,"

She only looked at me with a crazy look on her face that I couldn't describe. I know she cared about my well being and shit but, I wanted her to be concerned because she loved and cared about me. That was another battle for another day. Instead of telling her what was on my mind I got out the truck. I had barely taken four steps when I got a text telling me to come to a damn Black Tahoe with dark tint. After scanning the parking lot, I headed to the car. The problem I had was that I didn't know what dude looked like. I knew he knew me though. The reason I didn't want him to tell me was because I wanted to know how bad he needed whatever he was looking for. In this business you never make a call without knowing something about the person you're calling. I sat and waited for him to approach me first. I had my heat on me just in case he moved funny. Ciana had hers too I'm sure with her violent ass.

"Jabril, what up man?" A dude said as the door to the Tahoe opened. We shared a dap then I walked to the passenger side to get in.

"How you know Ali?" I asked getting to the point.

Ali was one of my closest friends at one point in my life. He was very private and kept his family and friends cut off from the street shit that he did. We were all that way back then that was one of the things that we picked up from Big Ten. Although Ish and I were under his wing; he trusted Ali only so much. There was something that was keeping him from getting tight with Ali though. That was something that I could never understand. Ali banged with us eight times out of ten but, when we had meetings or met the guys that Big Ten considered on his level Ali was never with us. I never got around to asking him about it though. Maybe, I should've, Big Ten was a complicated man but, also a simple one. Things were never obvious but, when he explained the reasons for his actions the shit was basic as fuck.

"I was tight with one of his brothers. My name is Carlos," he said holding out his hand for me to shake. I just looked at the shit.

"What's the reason for the phone call?"

"I need some tools just like I said. I'm not looking for crates of shit but, I definitely need a variety of shit. I need it for," he started to say but, I held up my hand stopping him mid-sentence.

"I don't want to know shit but, what you need. I don't give a fuck what you do with it as long as it doesn't lead back to me if you're on some fuck shit. You don't look like a terrorist or no shit like that so as long as what you want ain't crazy I might can help. It's a good thing you caught me when you did; I'm about to be done with this shit," I told him. He shifted in his seat. He was looking out of the windows and shit. What the fuck did he have to be nervous about? This is why I needed to look at his ass. His energy was off as fuck. "What the fuck is up with you being all shifty and shit? Are you okay?" I asked.

I wanted him to know I noticed his nervousness.

"Yeah, I'm good. I just didn't expect us to sit here basically talking about nothing," he said with a nervous smirk on his face.

"Oh, you were expecting me to just ride around with a bunch of guns in the car or something? I'm trying to understand what the fuck ya problem is," I told him.

"Problem? I don't have a problem, man are we gonna talk business or not?" he said forcefully.

I got out of the Tahoe and walked away. The vibe was off like a motherfucker. I heard him calling out to me but, I wasn't with whatever type of bullshit he's got going on. I've been doing this shit for a long time and I'll be damned if I get hemmed up on some bullshit. I got in the car to see Ciana looking at me all crazy.

"What's the look for?"

She looked at the guy I just got finished talking to then back to me. After shaking her head, she started the truck and pulled off.

"We need to talk later. It's important but, we can't talk right now. Is it okay if Iyanna stays with you tonight?" She asked.

"Yeah, you know she can stay whenever. Are you okay? You seem a little off right now," I told her.

"We'll talk later," was all she said.

"Are you ready baby girl? What do you want to do first?" I asked.

"I wanna go to kung fu panda!"

"Kung fu panda, isn't that a movie?" I asked confused.

"She's talking about Panda Express. She loves that place even though she can't get the name right. I tell her all the time what the real name is but she still calls it king fu panda," Ciana revealed.

I could only shake my head. Iyanna was always doing some

shit that you would never think of. I've never been to the place so I was at the mercy of my five year old. My stomach and head started hurting just thinking about what this little girl was gonna have my ass eating.

"What kind of food do they serve? I can't be eating no panda food. I'm a grown ass man. What are you gonna order for me baby girl?"

"Daddy you're funny. People can't eat panda food. They have people food. Stop being silly daddy," Iyanna said laughing.

"What kind of people food? Do they have steaks and macaroni and cheese? Is that the people food they have?" I asked.

I loved being silly with Iyanna she loved it when we did silly stuff. I just want her to laugh and be happy all of her life. If I had to ask questions that I already know the answer to and act surprised about shit I knew was gonna happen before it did then that's what I'll be doing until I take my last breath. My daughter was everything to me and it's times like these that she's the only one that matters.

"No daddy, they have noodle, rice, more noodle, and chicken. They have vegetables too but I just put those to the side," she said.

"You're supposed to eat those,"

"I tried it but it didn't do nothing for me," she sassed shaking her head from side to side. She was a mess and she knew it.

"If you want me to eat what you order for me you have to eat ya vegetables. You gotta build up your strength to keep those boys away," I told her.

"Oh no my stomach hurts. Every time daddy talks about those ugly boys my stomach hurts," she said holding her stomach. I looked at Ciana she just shook her head.

"So extra," Ciana said laughing.

This is what I wanted my days to look like in the future. Just me and my family happy as fuck and chilling. I know our time was coming but, I wanted it to start tomorrow even though I knew there was work that needed to be done before hand. Time waits for no one; it was time for me to start working on getting out of the streets and getting my family back. I needed that to be my reality from now on.

CHAPTER 6

iana

My stomach had been doing somersaults all day. My mind was racing with all kinds of scenarios that never ended well. The good thing was that Iyanna was worn out from today's activities. It took me no time to give her a bath and get her settled in her room at her dad's house. This gave us enough time to sit down and talk about what I had to say to him. I just hope he doesn't go off too bad. Once I made sure she was sleep and took her clothes out for tomorrow I turned off her light, closed the door and prepared for this conversation. When I got into the living room he was looking at something on TV.

"What's on your mind?" He asked me.

"What were you and the guy meeting about today?" I asked as I sat down.

"Guns, what's up man? You've been off all day,"

"I know him; well I think I know him. I only caught a glimpse of him when y'all dapped each other up. I only saw him from the side. Is his name Carlos?" I asked him.

Jabril cut the TV off and sat up in his seat. We looked at each other for what felt like an hour before the questions started.

"Know him how? I ain't never seen his ass before, that much I know. Y'all used to fuck or something," he said and my face instantly balled up. Carlos wasn't ugly but, he gave me this weird ass vibe all the time. It wasn't that I didn't like him but, he was someone that I definitely avoided if I could. "Ciana, I know you hear me talking to you," he said looking like he wanted to stand up.

"He's friends with Akeem. He was at the house just before Akeem left to go out of town. I thought they were going out of town together. A little bit before he came, Akeem had called me. We talked for a little bit but, before we got off the phone he said something to me about putting gas in the truck. I had this weird feeling come over me like he was somewhere watching me. I looked at Iyanna for a few minutes but, when I turned back around I saw the side of his face. My gut told me it was him but, I was hoping that I was wrong. I knew that if I told you then that you would want to kick his ass. We don't need you getting locked up,"

He just sat there. He was sitting straight up with his elbows on his knees, eyes closed.

"Does Akeem have a brother?"

"Yes, he had four but now he only has three,"

"What happen to the other one? What was his name?" He asked.

It wasn't the question that gave me pause but, it was the emotions that came through with each word as he said it. I could hear the pain although I had no idea where the pain was coming from. His leg was shaking and one hand was squeezing the other hand that was in a tight fist.

"He had a brother but he died in some deal gone bad. I don't know what happened but, he's always talking about how he's gonna get the guy back that his brother was working with," I told him.

Jabril stood to his feet and started pacing.

"How could I not know that they were brothers? I said that nigga looked familiar. I should've seen it, fuck, I should've seen it," he mumbled. Then he stopped and looked at me. "I need you and Iyanna to move in here. That nigga Akeem is trying to get at me behind his brother. He doesn't know the other shit his brother was into. You gotta move here until I figure out how to get at him before he gets to me. He's trying to use you to get to me but, that shit is dead. I'll kill his ass in front of a police station before I let anything happen to y'all," he said so fast it took me a minute for my ears to catch up with what he was saying.

"Hold up what are you talking about?" I asked simply because I hoped he wasn't saying what I thought he was saying.

"Ya man is talking about me. His brother Ali used to be my homie. We go back like a Cadillac on four flats. We were more like street brothers though. He only knew Ish was my brother because Ish used to run with us. Outside of that we didn't know shit about each other's families. I knew he had siblings and shit but, nothing specific. Shit was so fucked up that night," he paused looking at me. "If I would've known that this shit was gonna get brought to your front door I wouldn't have agreed to the shit. Now you and baby girl are involved all bets are off," he said shaking his head.

"You're talking in circles. What bet? Just tell me what the hell is going on,"

"You want a drink? You may just need a drink with the shit I'm about to drop on you," he said.

I watched as he walked in the kitchen to get a bottle and two glasses. I continued to focus on him as he poured our drinks.

"Tennison Overton is also known as Big Ten. He took me, Ish,

Ali, and this guy named Mike under his wing when we were young as fuck. Over the years Ish and I became more like sons to him. Ali and Mike were still around but, they were never around for the important more detailed shit. I still don't fully understand why but, now that I think of it. He didn't trust them like he trusted us. Big Ten wasn't just your average street kingpin. He was a man that knew people that we would never dream of knowing. I'm talking about Senators, Governors, owners of shit buildings and businesses that you would never think of like prisons and hospitals. He was well connected and had been as long as I've known him. A few years before he died he had a meeting with Ish and I to let us know that he had cancer and was dying. At first I thought he called us in there because he wanted us to take over. Come to find out he wanted us to get out and go legit. He had agreed to help finance our exit as long as we didn't get back in the shit after we left it completely. We didn't need his money because we had shit saved up. He knew that already so he put the money in a trust for our kids. He also made us promise not to tell anyone anything that was discussed.

"To make a long story short Ish got out and I slowly started making my exit. I eventually got out of everything else and was only running guns. At one point I was supplying most of the states on the east coast with guns. I can even get my hands on missile launchers. A couple of years ago I decided to tell Ali that I was getting out and going legit. I didn't tell him my reasons were you and Iyanna but, I told him that I wanted to settle down and have a family. I was in the process of introducing him to all of my suppliers and shit. I didn't want there to be any hiccups during the switch over. The thing I didn't know was that Ali and his stupid ass cousin were trying to play both sides. They were trying to play the suppliers against each other to get the guns for a cheaper price. Ali left me in the blind the whole time. I was walking around vouching for his ass and he's out here trying to play grown ass men. The one thing you don't do is play with a man's money. His little scheme was working until he tried to get greedy. Ali didn't know that although the suppliers were obviously in competition with each other they did communicate with one another randomly. It could be that they would call a meeting or maybe even see each other at a social event. They all ran in the same circles. To the naked eye these were respectable men in the community. The general public didn't know that they were also criminals.

"I didn't know any of the back and forth was going on with Ali and the suppliers. I also didn't know that Ali's stupid ass cousin was talking to the fucking feds. I never got the chance to ask Ali if he knew what his cousin was up to. The story I got was that his cousin got caught fucking some broad at a park one night in the car. Being that they were in the park after hours and fucking gave the cops probable cause to search the car. His dumb ass had liquor, weed, and some cocaine in there. To make matters worse the chick was seventeen. They locked his punk ass up. I doubt if he was in there for an hour before he started singing. I don't know how long or who he actually told on. What I do know is that I didn't kill either of them. I got a call saying the meeting was postponed behind some bullshit ass family emergency. Two days later I find out that Ali and his cousin were killed," he told me.

"Why does Akeem think Ali was with you?" I asked.

"I was supposed to be at the meeting. No one knows I wasn't there but the people that were actually there,"

"Why not just tell him what the fuck really happened? It doesn't make sense for all of this to go this far. If you weren't there then Akeem needs to know that," I told him.

"That nigga is not trying to hear that. If he's trying to set my black ass up by using you and some nigga I don't even know if me calling him is gonna change his mind,"

I understood where he was coming from but we had to figure out something. I couldn't lose him behind some bullshit that he didn't have anything to do with.

"We gotta figure out how to get his ass before he gets us,"

"Us? He only trying to kill my ass," Jabril said with a smirk.

That smirk let me know that he had officially checked out of the serious conversation that we were just having. Just that quick his mind took a nosedive in the gutter.

"Don't go there. We're not on that level but, I do care if you live or die," I confessed.

He stepped closer to me licking his lips.

"What if he standing outside waiting on me to come out? Just let me get a kiss from you so I can die a happy man, "this fool said.

"Jabril, move back with all that," I said to his hard head ass.

He kept walking up on me until he was damn near standing on top of my feet.

"All I asked for was a kiss Ciana. It ain't like I asked for what I really want from yo sexy ass,"

His lips touched mine. Even though that first touch was just a light one, it caused my knees to get weak. My mind told me to walk away but, my feet weren't moving. His hands cupped my face as he kissed me with a deeper urgency than before. His tongue was exploring every inch of the inside of my mouth getting reacquainted very well. A light moan escaped from my mouth. This is not where I thought I would end up tonight at all. The sound of someone clearing their throat caused us to stop the kiss and see who it was.

CHAPTER 7

abril

This bitch was gonna make me melt her ass in here tonight.

"What the fuck is going on here?" Porsche asked with her hands on her hip.

"How the fuck you get in here? You left your key the last time you left," I said to her, wrong time, wrong house, and wrong nigga to come at, ass.

"I asked you a question. You can't just skip around it like what I asked didn't matter," she said with much attitude.

"Man, you saw the shit with ya own two eyes what the fuck did it look like to you? What you want a damn play by play. How the fuck you get in here?" I asked.

"I have more than one key to your house, duh. This bitch couldn't wait until I left I see," she said rolling her eyes.

"Aye, I'm not gonna keep checking you about how the fuck you speak about Ciana. You need to stop rolling your eyes like that. You know you're one of those barbie built bitches. One of them damn thangs gonna roll right out ya head. I'm glad you're here you need to get all your shit and take it back to your house," I told her.

"You got me fucked up. We're not over, Jabril. We can't be over," she said.

"Why the fuck not?" I asked.

I was watching Ciana out of the corner of my eye. She could think she was gonna leave because this dumb broad was here but, it wasn't happening tonight. If anybody was leaving it was gonna be Porsche's plastic ass.

"You're gonna be a daddy!" She said with a big ass smile on her face.

"Yeah, I'm out," Ciana said.

"Bye baby mama," Porsche said.

"Can you tell this bitch that I'm two minutes off her ass? She's gonna keep playing with me and I'm gonna kick her ass all the way back to Germany with the rest of the Volkswagens," Ciana said as she walked past me.

"Hold up, Ciana you can't leave. I wasn't playing about what we just talked about. You and babygirl need to stay here until we get that shit cleared up," I told her as I held on to her hand.

"I thought she had a man to protect her ass. Why the fuck does she need to stay here?" Porsche asked.

Ciana jerked her hand away from me and stomped her mad ass down the hallway. I was pissed too because if this plastic bitch wouldn't have come in here I would be elbows deep in the one pussy I was craving. I ran my hand down from my forehead to my chin three times before I turned to Porsche.

"When did you find out you were pregnant man? Is it mine?" I asked her.

"I can't believe you would ask me some shit like that of course it yours. I would never step out on you," she said.

The sincerity in her voice didn't reach her eyes. I knew she was lying about not cheating on me so I seriously had doubts that the baby was mine if there was a baby in the first place. I just never cared enough to let her know that I knew. It was amazing how I could talk to her and treat her the way I do and she still be down behind my ass. She was either dumb as the plastic that her body parts were made of or she had a damn agenda. It seems like everyone had an agenda these days. The only people I could trust fully were Ish, Bali, Ciana, and Iyanna. I see that now. That fact alone was going to make the process of me getting out harder than I thought it was going to be.

"Come on let's go," I told Porsche.

"Where are we going?" She asked.

"Just bring your ass,"

"Are you going to leave her here alone? Why does she get to stay here while you're not here?" She asked.

I knew why she was so adamant about finding out why I chose to leave Ciana there. It took me months to leave Porsche in the house alone. Before that every time I left, her ass had to get up and leave too. She was visiting me not the house so if I wasn't there then that meant there wasn't a point of her being in the house. She used to get pissed about that shit. I remember one day I left her ass standing on the porch. She thought her standing there crying about how she didn't want to go to her place and me not trusting her was gonna change my mind. Truthfully, I don't trust her, I don't think I ever did. Just like I said there was something not right about her still being so in love with me after I talk to her the way I do. I pulled up at the drug store and parked she immediately started laughing.

"Get your ass out," I told her.

"I can't believe that you can't trust my words that I'm pregnant. You act like I'm some jump off. We are a fucking couple but, you don't believe me when I say I'm pregnant. What type of bullshit are you on?" She asked.

"The question is what type of bullshit are you on. You are fighting to be with a nigga that obviously doesn't want you. For months we've been arguing about stupid shit. I admit I did the shit on purpose thinking that your ass would up and leave. You not budging though and I need to know why," I told her. Now at this moment we are both sitting in the car. Even though I told her to get out she was still sitting in the passenger seat crying. The crying that she was doing had nothing to do with me taking her to the drug store to take a pregnancy test. She was crying about what she's been hiding. "What you crying for? If you're pregnant then you're pregnant," I told her.

"Jabril I love you," she said through her sobs.

"No, you don't. You're hiding something and it ain't got nothing to do with a baby. This is your chance to tell me what the hell is going on. After this moment if I find out that you're hiding something I'm gonna kill you. One shot to the forehead no questions asked. If you want me to hear your side then you better come clean now," I told her.

I looked at her closely. She was looking everywhere but directly at me. Porsche had been moving flawed but, I was hoping that we didn't get to this point. I admit that Ciana was the first to bring shit to my attention about Porsche. At first I thought she was always saying it because she just didn't like her. When Ciana kept saying how Porsche was sneaky I peeped how her phone stayed on silent. I also saw the faces she would make at my daughter when she thought I wasn't looking. When we had functions, she would play the role of the perfect girlfriend but, I started to see right through that. I would sit back and just check out how she moved when we were around a bunch of people compared to how she would act when we were home chilling. The one thing that she wasn't acting or faking about was her hate for Ciana. I will be the first to admit that Ciana could be a bitch sometimes. However, when they first met she tried to be friends Ciana. Ciana being the blunt person that she is let Porsche know that she didn't trust her and called her a snake. After that they were at each other whenever they felt like it. The only thing that stopped a fight from happening is the fact that Iyanna was around most of the time. One of the things I've learned in life was that you could count your true friends on one hand. Most of the people you considered to be friends are really enemies that are just waiting on your downfall. That's how I viewed Porsche right now as a fucking enemy.

"I'm not hiding anything. Let's get this over with since you don't believe me,"

She hopped her lying ass out of the car. I laughed at how mad her ass was walking. If her ass was real it would be shaking like a bowl of jello. Instead the shit was as still as the sidewalk she was fast stepping on. Just as I was about to get out of the car my phone rang.

"You're late, I already know that Akeem is Ali's brother. The reason for all this bullshit is Akeem seems to think I killed Ali. It took you a while to figure that one out," I said.

"Yeah it took a little longer. I admit when I got the call from Ish it threw me off. You never have any issues because you don't let anyone get close enough to care about a background," Pete the nerdy computer guy said.

Pete was introduced to us as an Intern for the renovation company when Ish first started it. Partnering with a local community college to get some free labor and help the youth at the same time. Come to find out the nigga was smart as fuck with computers, stocks, and all the other shit that normal people paid no mind to. Ish knew more about the kid than I did. He was right I hated people getting close because there was nothing good that could come from someone knowing all about you and how you think about shit.

"There was something that came up that's the reason for the call. I don't know how to say this but, Porsche is Ali's ex-girlfriend. She talks to Akeem at least twice a week. They're also meeting randomly at hotels and shit," he said. That was all I needed to hear. That bitch and her nigga were both gonna die.

CHAPTER 8

 orsche

"Why are you calling me and you're supposed to be all hugged up with that nigga to get him comfortable enough to let his guard down." Akeem yelled at me.

"I know the damn plan Keem. I thought you were supposed to get close to the bitch since you want to talk about what I'm supposed to be doing. If you're doing your job why the hell is she at Jabril's house kissing all on him. If I wouldn't have come in they would have been fucking right there in his living room. Where the fuck are you?" I tried to whisper.

When I got out of the car I heard Jabril's phone ring. I didn't hear him walking behind me so that meant he was still on the phone. I rushed to the bathroom so I could make this call. Akeem always thought he had all the answers but, his stupid ass plan was falling apart and he didn't even know it.

"I'm handling something else. She thinks I'm out of town," he replied.

"You think she's home waiting on you and she's trying to

spread her legs for her baby daddy. You think you got her under control but, that's the shit you don't have," I told him.

"Where is Jabril while you're on the phone arguing with me?" He asked.

"What? He's in the car on the phone. Don't worry about me but, you need to get that bitch in line," I argued.

"You need to find out what you can and get back to me we're running out of time. Stop fucking around and get me what I need," he said before ending the call.

There was a knock on the door. I jumped because I didn't expect anyone to knock and I knew exactly who it was.

"Open the door man. I hope you're in there with a pregnancy test because I don't want to have to do this shit all over again," Jabril complained through the door.

"No, I don't have a test in here with me. You're the one that wants me to take it. You should be the one to pay for it,"

"Open the door before I kick it in. I got a test right here for you to take. This is the shit that you do. You knew why we were here so why the fuck are you in here without a damn test. Don't tell me your brain is plastic too," he continued.

I stood there looking at myself in the bathroom mirror. Jabril used to be funny, protective and genuinely concerned about me. Now here I am pregnant with a child that should've never been created with the love of my life's brother. Akeem has me mixed up in this bullshit because he wants revenge on something that he doesn't have all the details about. No matter how much I told him that I didn't think that Jabril killed Ali he swears I'm just saying it because I have feelings for Jabril. He'd repeatedly tell me that I don't know shit about the street. That may be true but, I do know a liar when I see one. Jabril hadn't lied to me so far so why would he lie now. No matter how hurtful the shit was Jabril always told the truth. Jabril thought that him calling me plastic and talking about all the surgeries would hurt my feelings. It never did because the surgeries weren't done for anyone but, myself. With the help of Ali I was now walking around with the body that I've always dreamed of. Jabril could joke and complain all he wanted to but, none of that mattered, I was enjoying being on his arm. All eyes were on me and that was the point. If Ali wouldn't have died he was going to take over what Jabril had going on anyway. Ali would always say that Jabril was only doing shit in the streets because he had ADD. Up until I spent time with Jabril I thought that he was just exaggerating. However, being around Jabril and his brother Ish I knew that Ali was right on the money with that. Jabril didn't need money, he wasn't out here trying to survive. He was in the streets because he was bored. That shit used to get on Ali's nerves because he felt like Jabril was taking up space when there were people out here who needed the streets to survive. Ali would say that he had respect for Jabril but, he was just taking up space in the game.

I missed Ali more and more every day. Me getting with Akeem was never the plan. Akeem had come over to check on me about four months after Ali had been killed. It took me a long time to climb out of the depression that Ali's death had put me in. That particular night I was home drinking and remembering all the good times that Ali and I shared. The knocking on the door caused me to jump in fear looking around.

"Damn it, I'm coming Jabril," I said shakily. I opened the door just for Jabril to hold a pregnancy test so close to my face that it was touching the tip of my nose. He was so disrespectful sometimes, well most of the damn time.

"Back up so you can pee on this shit and I can go back home," he said in a rougher tone than usual. He even bumped me a little as he walked past me to enter the ladies' room of the drug store.

"You do know you're in the ladies' room?" I asked.

"They don't have a bathroom for snakes. It ain't like we're in the zoo," he said.

"Snake? Are you calling me a snake?"

"Man, piss on the stick so we can leave," he said brushing my question off.

"Why can't I just use the bathroom at your house? She's gonna find out about the baby anyway. It might as well be known; that way by the time I have the baby she'll understand her place in your life," I told him as I went into the stall and tried to close the door. He pushed the door back open with his hand.

"Nah, I don't trust shit you do that I don't see with my own eyes,"

"If you have something to say then just say it,"

I was tired of him talking in circles. He's been giving off this weird ass vibe since I opened the bathroom door. Before he was always giving off an asshole vibe but, now it was more anger showing through than anything. I sat the test on the back of the toilet and stood there waiting and too scared to come out of the stall totally. There was a knock on the door. Jabril kissed his teeth then went to open the door.

"On some real shit we busy up in here. Use the other bathroom. I know it says the men's room but, you're old as shit so it doesn't matter to you if you see somebody's dick or not. Either that or you can wait until this test pop up with the answer. Once we get the answer you can have the bathroom it's up to you, Blanche," Jabril said followed by him closing the door and locking it.

"Did you call that lady Blanche?" I asked.

"How much longer do we have?" He asked.

"You're making me feel like you don't want to be here," I told him.

"I don't," he said shrugging his shoulders.

I refuse to sit here and keep subjecting myself to this stupid ass attitude that he has. I know I'm not the reason for him acting like this. We were standing in the bathroom looking like two assholes right now. We could've gone to his house but, he wanted to keep shit from his precious Ciana. That bitch was gonna have to move the fuck over because a new and improved baby mama was about to step on the scene. I smiled as the second pink line started to show on the test. I picked it up with the biggest smile ever on my face.

"We're having a baby!" I said with so much energy.

He looked at me like he wanted to kill me and walked out of the bathroom.

CHAPTER 9

iana

Since him and the bitch left I toyed with packing up Iyanna and going home. When I thought about what we discussed about Carlos and Akeem I sat my ass back down. I didn't need Akeem finding out that Jabril and I knew some of what he was up to just yet. Of course, my phone started ringing when I was trying to figure out what my next move was going to be.

"Hello," I answered.

"Where the hell are you?"

"You're not here so that doesn't matter. Why do you want to know where I am?"

"Just answer the question. If I find out you're around your baby daddy's house me and you are gonna have a problem. I keep telling you that nigga wants you but, you keep acting like Stevie Wonder to the shit. That nigga wants you Ci," he fussed.

"Okay look, I don't know who the fuck you call yourself yelling at but, it sure as hell ain't me. You need to evaluate whatever the fuck it is that has you talking out of pocket to me," I told him.

Akeem knew damn well he was doing too much by raising his voice at me. I didn't yell at his ass so he needed to check that shit.

"Are you fucking that nigga?" He asked instantly pissing me off.

"Are you out of town or did you lie to me about going?" I asked.

"Why are you trying to change the subject? Are you fucking your baby daddy?" He asked again.

"No, I'm not but, since you're down my back about it I will tonight. Fuck you Akeem," I told him before ending the call.

How the fuck is he calling me trying to question me? He was the one working on some flawed shit.

"Are you okay?" Jabril asked.

I didn't hear him come in the house. Why was he being a creep right now, not letting me know he was standing there? He had a faraway look in his eye. I hadn't seen him with this look before. It was alarming to me that he was throwing off these weird vibes right now. He stepped inside the room.

"What's wrong?" I asked.

"She's pregnant but, I doubt it's mine," he said low as fuck.

"Okay, it's not like the world is over. What has you looking like that?" I asked.

"She's connected to Akeem. When I say connected I mean that the baby might be his even though she used to fuck with Ali," he said dropping the bomb on me.

"Huh? Ali and Akeem are brothers right. That's what you said earlier. Is she in on whatever it is that he has going on to get at you? What the fuck is really going on out here in these streets?" I asked.

"Yeah, how much more fucked up news can I handle? I wanted to kill her ass when we went to the drug store. She was standing there waiting on the test to be ready. Her ass had no clue that I was picturing all the ways that I could kill her the entire time. I was going to kill her when I first got off the phone with Pete. Iyanna saved her ass for the time being," he said shaking his head.

I sat there trying to digest what he just told me. Was there anyone that we were around that was legit? This is getting ridiculous.

"He was just on the phone asking if we were fucking. Then you come in here telling me that he might be that bitches baby daddy. It never fails niggas always want more than what they have. I hated getting invested in people just for them to hurt me. This shit is for the birds. I might go gay after this," I told him.

"Go gay?"

"Yeah, niggas can't stay faithful to save their lives!"

"Aye, you talk that shit about him. I never cheated on your ass when we were together," he said looking at me like I was crazy.

"That's what your mouth says. I'm not talking about you anyway. Stop taking everything personal. We're not together so there's no need for us to have this conversation," I told him.

"Well let it be known that I didn't do your ass dirty."

"Whatever, why are you so pressed on that anyway?"

"Just give me my props on that shit. He's stupid as fuck to be doing the shit that he's doing. It's no surprise to me that he's cheating. Dumb niggas do dumb shit. You deserve better."

"Yeah, okay. If I deserve better than why is everyone wasting my time. Life is short. At this rate I'll never get married. I'm doomed to be a baby mama."

"Ciana, you'll be a wife one day watch what I say," he said.

"Okay Jabril," I said laughing.

"Any man would cherish you even though your mouth can be reckless as hell. You have a beautiful heart and soul," he said looking at me.

There was something else going on in his head. I could see it all in his eyes. It wasn't just what Akeem had going on that was bothering him. We may not be together but, we know each other very well.

"You a little emotional tonight, you should take a shower and go to bed," I told him.

"Nah, I have some shit that I need to say. Ciana we should've worked out," he said I stood to my feet. I didn't want to go down this road with him tonight. We agreed to just co-parent and we had to live with that decision there was no going back.

"Not tonight, Jabril, I don't feel like it."

"Nah, we're doing this right now. I don't want there to be any misunderstanding going on between us. Do you even remember why we agreed to just co-parent? I know you don't because I don't either. It was like one day we were together and then we weren't. I ran into Porsche and you went with Akeem. What if this was their plan all along? What if us meeting them wasn't just a coincidence? Think about it. If they are a couple like Pete says then they could be with us just to take me down. If that's the case then you and Iyanna are in danger because of me?"

I sat back down beside him and took his face in my hands.

"None of this is on you. You didn't kill Ali so how can any of this be on you? We are gonna get through this. None of us are going to get hurt either," I told him.

"Life is too short for all this shit. This is gonna get worse before it gets better. I want you to know I love you," he told me.

"I have love for you too Jabril."

"Nah, you're not hearing me. Ciana, I love you, I'm in love with you. I have been since before our first night together. You make my heart speed up depending on the situation. If you're fussing and cursing then I know you're fine. When you're not I'm on high alert. Your smile makes me smile. The way you moan when you bite into a fresh pineapple makes my dick hard. The way you suck on a crab leg causes me to have flash backs of the night and next day that we fucked nonstop. Porsche is just a place holder for the one woman who holds my heart and gave birth to my child," he said looking at me with tears in his eyes.

"Jabril, you can't be talking like that because of what you're going through right now. That's no reason for you to think you're in love with me. There's a difference between being in love and having love for someone," I told him.

My heart was beating so fast and loud that I know he had to hear it. Why couldn't I just tell him that I loved him too? This man was the father of my child but, I couldn't find the words to tell him how I really felt. I cursed myself for acting like some punk ass schoolgirl.

"Say it Ciana," he said looking at me.

"Say what?" I asked knowing damn well what he was talking about. He shook his head and let out a low chuckle. I watched as he ran his hand from his forehead down the length of his face. He blew out a breath then chuckled again. "Jabril you're acting like a mental patient," I told him.

"Love does that shit to niggas I guess,"

He collapsed his mouth over mine. I wanted to back up but, my body didn't move. I wanted to get up slap him and walk out of the room. Instead, my body surrendered to this man. I could feel my nipples harden just from the sensual kiss that he was giving me. We weren't touching in any other way than with our mouths but, my panties were getting more soaked as the kiss continued. Finally, I got the power to stop the kiss. I was breathing heavy and trying to understand why this man always drove my body crazy.

"You have a pregnant girlfriend. I have a boyfriend," I said as I held my hand up.

"Nice try," he said as he forced me to lay down on the bed.

He was feeling and kissing all on me. It wasn't in a way that made me feel anything other than the love that he professed to have. The touch of his skin on mine cause tingles to vibrate through my body. "Can I have you tonight?" He whispered in my ear. I was trying to answer him but, his hand was currently passing my navel and heading towards my extremely moist pussy. My eyes were closed because this had to be another dream that I was experiencing right now. "Open your eyes and look at me. Keep them shits open too," he whispered in my ear. He was testing me right now. This is what Jabril loved to do. He got off on pushing me to my limit. I felt his large middle finger slide between my pussy lips. He licked his lips as he watched me watch him. "Damn she ready like a mother fucker," he said. I could feel my eyes closing involuntarily. "Open them eyes up," he commanded as he pinched my clit. My eyes shot up looking at him with that sexy ass smirk on his face.

"Jabril," I moaned out but, it sounded more like a whine to me.

"That's not how you say it," he said pinching my clit once again.

"Shit," I said as he started playing with my pussy with two fingers instead of one. My orgasm was coming and I needed to close my eyes but, I knew if I did that he would pinch me again. He knew that I was about to climax as well because before I could release he was face deep in my pussy wanting to catch every drop of my climax with his mouth. He was still looking at me which made the climax even more impactful. I was in for a long night because the last time I saw that look in his eye we made Iyanna.

CHAPTER 10

abril

I had her ass right where I wanted her. I was gonna do everything I could to knock her ass up tonight. It was fucked up of me to do this to her tonight but, I needed to be inside her. There wasn't gonna be a condom or anything else depriving me of the smooth, silky, warm, wet grip of her pussy. I stared her down as I ate her pussy like it was some strawberry cake, which is my favorite cake. She was fighting to keep her eyes on me which only turned me on even more. Ciana loved to be in control. However, when her and I were in the bedroom no matter how much time passed I was always gonna be the fucking boss, literally.

She kept her eyes on me as she started playing with her nipples and licking her lips. She must want to get knocked up tonight. I slid my sweatpants down to pull my hard dick out. It had been so long since I tasted a pussy I didn't want to stop eating. I couldn't fuck her and eat her at the same time so I had to pull my mouth away from my favorite place. I eased up to kiss her as I slid my dick inside her. I ended up sliding in with too much force.

"Ahhh!" She screamed out. Instead of apologizing I eased out and slammed back inside her with more force than before.

"Stop fucking playing with me Ciana," I told her through gritted teeth as I continued my assault on her pussy. She was still looking at me but, I was determined to break her down from the inside out on this damn day.

"Jabril, what are you doing?" She pleaded with tears in her eyes.

"I'm fucking loving your hardheaded ass, that's what I'm doing,"

I could feel her walls contracting squeezing the life out of my dick. I didn't want to cum just yet but, I know she needs to. I dropped to my knees quick as fuck to eat my pussy some more. The way I was driving her crazy right now that nigga Akeem couldn't be fucking my baby the right way. She was gonna sleep for damn near two days when I got finish loving on her like a real nigga is supposed to. She gripped my head with her hands as she screamed out with sexual pleasure. Before she could get all of that orgasm out I was back in her face and dick deep up in her. She wrapped her legs around my waist with her nails digging deeper into my skin with each stroke. I was sweating my ass off but, if I was gonna have a damn heart attack, right now the shit would be very well worth it.

"Oh god, oh god!"

"You calling other niggas while I'm in this?" I asked her.

"Shit," she called out.

I put my feet on the floor while I was still inside her. I grabbed both of her ankles and held her legs as far apart as they would go. Our eyes were still connected which was fine with me.

"Play with that motherfucker," I told her.

She did as she was told. I admit I was a freak most of the time but, when it came to Ciana I was on a different level. The freakiest shit that I did with Porsche was fucking in the kitchen. Even then she was bent over so I wouldn't have to look at her. With Ciana I wanted to see every fuck face she made while I was inside her. I didn't want to miss shit. It was crazy how she made me feel things that I've never felt before. There was no way she was gonna leave me and not know that she was my forever. All this bullshit going on had to pass, there was no way that it couldn't. We were going to be here to raise our children together. Damn what Akeem and Porsche had going on. It was all about our family from here on out. I guess my thoughts took control because Ciana was screaming bloody murder right now.

"Jabril, Jaaaaaaa," she yelled.

That's only part of what I wanted to hear. I continued to pump in and out of her with all the might in me that I had.

"That's not what I want to hear," I said sounding winded but still giving her every ounce of me.

"I do Jabril, I do, shit,"

"Do what Ciana? What the fuck do you do? Tell me got damn it,"

"I ... I ... I love you Jabril with all that I am!" She yelled.

That right there is what I wanted to know. I released all of our future kids inside of her. Once I was empty I collapsed on the bed beside her. We were both breathing heavy but, that shit was music to my ears. I heard her sniffling. She ain't have no reason to cry though. We were locked in now, that's for damn sure.

)()()()(

While Ciana slept I went to check on my baby girl. I know she heard all that noise that me and her mama made last night and this morning. Peeking my head into her room she was already up looking at TV.

"What are you doing in here little one?"

"Daddy, I haven't been a little one since I started tying my shoes and using the bathroom on my own. Are me and mommie going to live here now?" She asked.

"Slow down what happen to good morning. You just can't start your morning off with questions. You're gonna have to ask your mama that one though. I do know y'all will be here for a couple of weeks. Do you want to live here?" I asked.

"Yes, I'll talk to mommie so we can look at the options," she said sound like a grown woman.

"What do you know about options?" I asked making her giggle.

"Uncle Ish always tells me to look at the options when I ask him can I do something or I ask him to buy something. He says options are going to help me make better choices," she said smiling all big like she had won a present just by answering me.

"That's good, I guess you and mommy are going to have to look at the options. Are you ready for breakfast?" I asked.

"No, I can wait for mommy to wake up. I don't want cereal and that's all you know how to make,"

"I know how to fix more than cereal," I told her acting like I was hurt.

"Hot dogs and sandwiches don't count," she giggled.

I laid in the bed with her for a while looking at all the dumb ass cartoons that she likes to watch. It wasn't about what was on the TV though it was about spending some down time with my babygirl. I had now saw things in a different light since leaving the drug store last night. The one thing I do know is that Porsche couldn't be having a kid by me. Ciana was gonna have all my kids' period. After falling asleep with baby girl, I woke up in her bed alone. She had put this big ass teddy bear in the bed when she got out. I shook my head at how much she's grown up. I wasn't ready for her to get older. I wanted her to stay my baby for the rest of her life.

I found her and her mother in the kitchen cooking breakfast. I stayed out of their sight for a little bit just taking in the view of my world playing around in the kitchen more than they were cooking. Seeing Ciana with Iyanna was enough to bring a nigga to his knees at the thought of losing them. I couldn't live if anything happened to them. They were my everything and I had to protect them at all costs. I chose to go in my office instead of interrupting them in the kitchen. I called Ish because I had to get a conclusion to this situation quick as hell.

"Hello,"

"I need your help with something. I decided that I'm gonna go 'head and lock Ciana's ass down. I'm not talking about us going together or us living together. I'm gonna marry her man she's it for me. I gotta be here for her and the kids. I can't do that with me being in the streets or with Akeem trying to kill my ass," I said all in one breath. I waited for him to respond but, was greeted by the beeping sound letting me know that his ass had ended the call on me. I called him right back.

"What year is it and who's the president?" He asked when he answered the call.

"Nigga, it's 2020 and Trump's orange headed ass is the president. That doesn't have shit to do with what I told you before you ended the call on my ass," I told him.

"Oh, I heard your ass and I have motherfucking questions. First of all, how the hell you gonna marry someone that you're not with? Second, last I heard you only had Iyanna so why the fuck did you put an s on the word kid? Lastly, What the fuck you mean Akeem is trying to kill you?" He barked.

I gave him the run down on the situation with Akeem not

leaving out the fact that Porsche is mixed up in this shit or the fact that she claims to be pregnant by me. He was quiet as hell the entire time I was talking. I had to get some input from him because although he can be more deadly than me he's the one of us that's the thinker. I wanted to just go hunt the nigga down and put a bullet in his ass but, I had a family to think about.

"Oh yeah, stop talking to my kid about looking at all the options and shit. She sounds like an old ass lady talking about that shit," I laughed.

"I should've talked to you about looking at all your damn options then you wouldn't be out here trying to marry a woman that you're no longer with and having a kid with a woman that you don't want to be with. Here it is early as fuck and you have me in my office taking shots. You're stressing me the fuck out," he said sounded stressed.

"I wasn't talking about Porsche when I said kids," I told him. I was about to explain but, he started going in on my ass.

"Nigga, you gonna be out here just shooting up anybody with ya damn kids. Come on bro we don't move like that. That's reckless as fuck. You're gonna fuck around and when you die we're gonna have to get three family cars for all the kids and baby mama's your ass out here trying to have. What the fuck man? Who's the new bitch that you got pregnant? I hope she ain't white that's all we need is her white ass coming over here with all this black art that Bali is decorating the house with," he was straight going off.

"Man shut all that shit up. I was talking about Ciana. Hopefully, I knocked her ass up again last night," I told him. I could tell that he was still on the phone but, it was quiet as shit right now. "Man, say something your ass was just going in on me," I told him laughing at how quick he shut all that shit up.

"Always gotta do shit the hard way. All you had to do was let her know how you felt a long time ago. Both of y'all are made for each other hardheaded as fuck. Lord let me pray over Iyanna. I'm gonna need her to listen to others more than her parents do," he said.

"Yeah, you've been around Bali too damn much. Stop being so damn dramatic. Everybody can't fall in love and all that fah-la-la-la shit like you and Bali," I told him.

"You got jokes and shit. What are you gonna do about Akeem's ass?"

"Kill his ass what the fuck you thought this was," I told him.

"Oh, you talking like you have a plan," he said with a chuckle.

"I do big bruh, I do,"

"Oh shit, well share that shit with me," he said.

I leaned back in my chair and told him exactly what I had in mind.

CHAPTER 11

keem

"This bitch is gonna make me kill her ass," I mumbled to myself.

I had been calling Porsche for the past three hours only for her ass not to answer. She was all upset and shit because I got on her ass for telling that nigga that the baby was his. I understood why she did it but, being that she felt like they weren't going to get back together she did it for nothing. Here her ass is now calling me back. I swear if this is how her hormones are going to be I'll kill the baby my damn self.

"What the fuck is your problem now? You need to tighten up and stop acting so damn extra all the fucking time," I said when I answered the phone.

"Fuck you Akeem; you're not the one carrying a child by your dead man's brother. You keep asking me to do all this stuff but, when I do it you have a damn problem. I had to tell him about the baby or he would've cut me off free and clear. Now that he thinks I'm carrying his child he has to deal with me even if he doesn't like me much right now," she explained.

"All that might be true but, I don't trust his ass. Shit, I barely trust you. As for you being knocked up by your dead ex's brother, you should've thought about that shit before you put my dick in your mouth," I told her before ending the call.

Dealing with her was starting to get exhausting as fuck. She claimed that fucking with me was the wrong thing to do but, she was always wanting to fuck me when we were around each other. She was the most confusing female I've ever known. Ciana was confused too but, she wasn't as annoying with it as Porsche is. Ciana still loved that nigga but, wanted to hurt him by not being with him. Her stubbornness just opened the door for me to slide in, feed her some bullshit, do a few things to make her fall head over heels for me then use her ass as bait to get at Jabril. I wonder how she would react if she knew that half of the time my dick was hard just from thinking about killing her baby daddy. It's wild as hell to be fucking the baby mama of the man you're daydreaming about killing. I can say that those times are the most powerful nuts that I've ever experienced.

"So, when the baby comes is the baby going to call you Uncle-Daddy?" Carlos asked with a laugh.

"I see you got jokes. Don't worry about what the fuck I got going on outside of what the endgame is. What Porsche and I do doesn't concern your ass so leave it be. Did he call you back yet?"

"No, I don't think he is. If he wanted to do business with me he would've called the day after we met up,"

"Are you sure you didn't say too much? It had to be something that spooked his ass. If you did anything to fuck this up I'll kill you," I told Carlos.

"Nigga fuck you. You're the one that wants my help not the other way around. You need to stop acting like I'm some kind of side kick or some shit. Give me my fucking respect," Carlos said.

This was the problem with motherfuckers they always felt that they could talk to you crazy because you 'need' them. Carlos knows damn well that he can't fight good enough to be talking all the big shit he's spitting right now. I didn't choose him to help me because I needed him. I chose him because he's expendable. I know once Jabril gets wind that he is setting him up then he's gonna kill Carlos. He might even get pissed enough with Porsche to kill her or at least beat the baby out of her. Shit, that nigga can tie up my loose ends before I kill him. That would work out perfectly. Too bad this isn't a damn movie or TV show because I know somethings gonna happen to fuck all of it up. "I know you fucking heard me," Carlos screamed at me.

I punched him in the mouth two times followed by a punch to the stomach. His ass hit the floor like a ton of bricks. I pressed my foot on his neck.

"Say that shit a little louder I can't hear you," I said as I pressed my foot harder on his damn neck. "I suggest you shut the fuck up and stop with all the extra shit.

I heard him coughing as I walked out of the room. He didn't understand but the next time I was going to kill his ass and figure out a plan B. The only man I ever needed was my damn brother, nothing's going to change that.

()()()()

"Ahh, ahh, yeah baby right there," she screamed.

I held her waist tighter because she kept running from my dick. She was fucking up my train of thought with all the screaming and shit. I know my dick game is the shit but, she's doing way too fucking much right now.

"Take this dick and shut the fuck up. Every time you get out of hand I gotta dig in ya shit so you can get some act right. The next time you talk out the side of your neck I'm gonna stick my dick down your throat," I said as I continued to fuck her. She was sure to not say anything but, she damn sure was humming her ass off right now. "Come catch this shit,"

She did as I told her, like always. She spun around fast to stick my dick in her mouth. She bobbed her head up and down less than ten times before I shot off in her mouth. I watched as she played with my cum in her mouth before swallowing it. One thing my brother surely knew was to find a damn freak. Porsche was definitely a freak. Her head game and willingness to do whatever, whenever, and whomever made all the dumb shit she said and did invisible.

"I really needed that," she said trying to get up under me.

"Yo, back up you got dick all on your breath,"

"It's your dick,"

"So, is that supposed to make it better. Don't be all in my face with dick on ya breath. That shit is disrespectful. When are you gonna try to get back in the house with that nigga?" I asked.

Hopefully the dick she just got calmed her ass down enough for us to have a positive conversation.

"I'm going over there after my nap. I bet your little girlfriend and the brat are still over there. I just want all of this to be done. Jabril needs to pay for taking Ali away from me. I think we should kill the bitch too. Maybe we can kill her first so he can undergo the pain he put us through."

"Just stick to the original plan. Don't start thinking because that's not gonna help."

"Are you calling me dumb?" She asked with a shocked look on her face.

"No, I said you thinking never helps the situation. If you feel like you're dumb then there ain't shit I can do about that," I told her. She kissed her teeth and rolled her eyes.

"Sounds like the same thing to me. Look once all this is over we don't have to be together. We can go our separate ways."

"I know you don't think that once all this shit comes out that Jabril is gonna be alive but, if he happens to live you and him are not gonna ride off into the sunset and live happily ever after. He's already kicked you to the curb. I still don't understand how you thought telling him you were pregnant was going to make him take you back. Do you not see all these single mothers out here? I bet you any amount of money that they tried that 'I'm pregnant' shit too and look where they ended up. That's a prime example of thinking gone wrong," I told her.

She was sitting there looking sad and shit. My phone rang with a picture of Ciana showing on the screen. Porsche mumbled some shit to herself because she wasn't talking to me. I looked at her in a way that let her know that she needed to shut the fuck up while I was on the phone.

"Hey babe," I answered

"Hey, I was just calling to check on you. I feel bad that our night didn't go as planned. We need a do over, don't you think?" She asked.

"You don't have to go through all of that. I'm good with coming to your house just to chill with you when I get back. I do feel kind of bad that I messed up your surprise. Anyway, weren't you just laying my ass out. The last time I talked you were at ya baby's daddy house. Where that nigga at while you calling me and shit? You gonna fuck around and have me fucking him up before it's all said and done," I told her.

"That didn't have anything to do with me. You called me talking all that shit. It wasn't about a damn thing that I did. I haven't given you a reason to think that Jabril and I are doing anything other than co-parenting. That part of us has been over and done with for a long time now. I can't keep doing this question and answer session with you just because you feel some type of way. If we're gonna be together then that's what we will be together. I'm not gonna keep doing this shit. Let me know now if you can't deal with him and I in communication all the time. It's not like we were just a couple that broke up we have a whole child to raise," she fussed.

I know she's right but, I can't tell her where I got that information from about her being at that niggas house in the first place. This shit wasn't supposed to take this long and it damn sure isn't supposed to be this complicated. I never thought that I would have feelings for Ciana. I didn't love her or no shit like that but, I don't want her with that nigga either. I don't know what the hell made her change her mind but, I was gonna try to get her to leave his ass totally. She didn't need his punk ass anyway.

"Okay so just call me when you're an hour away from the house. Iyanna's staying with her father while school is out. We can have the place to ourselves for the night. How does that sound to you?" She asked.

"It sounds good to me. Make sure you get some rest because I'm gonna wear your ass out when I get there."

"Trust me I'm ready for it baby. I'm not gonna hold you up from working. Call me later if you can."

"I'll call you in a few hours. You be safe out there in those streets," I told her before I ended the call. Porsche kissed her teeth again. "Get that shit off your chest then," I told her.

"You never told me to be safe out here. That's fucked up Akeem," she whined.

"Why would I tell you that when I really want you to go play in traffic? Weren't you leaving?" I asked her.

I watched as she gathered her shit up and left. I took a deep breath and laid across the bed. I could finally relax for the time being.

CHAPTER 12

orsche

My phone rang before I could get out of the hotel. I rolled my eyes at the fact that Jabril had basically kicked me to the curb for his bullshit ass family but, here he is calling me. Maybe, he was calling to let me know that we could get back together for the baby.

"Hello," I answered trying to sound sexy even though I was tired and walking across the parking garage in heels with swollen feet. I had to remember to call the doctor because there was no way that my feet swelling this early in the pregnancy was a good thing.

"I'm at your house but you're not here,"

"Okay great observation. Why are you at my house?"

"I had some time to think and we need to sit down and have a talk. I'm talking about a real talk not one where you scream, holler, and cry. If you're on that bullshit today I can just go home," he said.

"I can't talk to you right now call me back in a few days," I told him then ended the call. I looked up to see someone standing by my car. This day was just getting better and better. "Why are you out here?" I asked looking around.

"I know Mrs. Friendly Pussy isn't scared of the big bad wolf finding out about your supply of extra dick; are you?" He asked me.

"I told you that I was gonna try to see you today. Nowhere and in no other language does that translate into pop up on me. You have to keep playing this thing smart. Now is not the time to get sloppy," I said trying to talk some sense into him.

His mind was in other places though he wanted to rub on my stomach and shit. It did feel good to have someone excited for me to have this baby even though I presently have three different men thinking that it's theirs. A woman has to do what a woman has to do. Ali had my ass spoiled to the point where I've only worked for one week during my entire life. When he died I had nothing but the money in the bank to fall back on. I had to find a new sponsor pronto. It was a good thing that I was looking because I hit the jackpot two times over.

"How can I get sloppy? I've been in this shit for three years now. Neither one of them even know that I'm an undercover cop. I know you're not gonna say anything. We all know you haven't said a word since I've been paying for your mother to keep her house. I really need you to go there to stay with her before this all blows up in all of our faces," he told me.

"If Akeem doesn't get impatient everything will be fine. You just make sure he doesn't go off the deep end before it's time for him to die."

"You might be right about that. I just need for you to keep playing your part a little bit longer. Akeem still doesn't know that his brother was my CI for damn near four years. I've been trying to tell him that he needs to get some proof. If he finds that out then he'll start questioning everything. We don't need

Akeem questioning shit. You just keep playing your role. It won't be long now," he told me.

Carlos was playing a dangerous game and the longer it took for all this shit to end was making everything worse. I had been playing this role for so long that I was starting to forget who I really was outside of all this hood 007 shit. Truthfully in all these lies that were being told I doubted I wanted to be in a relationship with any of the three men that could possibly be my child's father. My heart still ached for Ali he was the man I had been waiting for. I suspected that Carlos had more to do with his murder than he tells me. He wasn't close as the others to Ali but, he could've warned him that night I'm sure. In all the role playing I didn't look into it at the time like I should've. Now that Jabril is pissed I don't have to be up under him as much. Akeem is still trying to appease Ciana's ass so he won't have time to hunt me down. I watched as Carlos got in his car then I got in mine. We were gonna play follow the leader today. If I find out that he could've stopped the murder but chose not to, I will kill him myself.

()()()()()()

After a day of following Carlos my head, heart, and soul were hurting. I drove around crying for only god knows how long. I found myself at the grave site of Ali. None of this was making sense. I knew that Carlos was involved but to see him not only dealing with me as an ex of Ali's; he visited another ex of Ali's. I know the bitch because I had to show her ass what these hands can do a time or two before. I instantly felt used and played to the fullest. Not only was he with this bitch but, he was out playing with her kids. I couldn't get close enough to see if the kids favored him but, the way he was interacting with them showed me that he was extremely close to them. Here it is everyone is beefing with each other behind Ali's death and he's just fucking all his ex-girlfriends.

"Why didn't you tell me that you weren't trusting Carlos? I know you had to know something. You were the one who always picked up on shit. You never warned me so I figured he was cool. I found out how wrong I was. It's sad to say that you're dead and everyone around you is looking flawed as fuck. Jabril is the only one in the dark from what I know. I'm so glad that you instilled in me to never show my entire hand when dealing with people. You didn't even show me your hand. Why didn't you just tell me what you were up to? I could've helped in some way I'm sure. I miss you so much. I know you're pissed about me and Akeem getting together well, we're not together but, you know what I mean."

"He might know what you mean but, I don't."

I turned around scared to death. It would be just my luck that he's been following me.

"What are you doing here?"

"I've been following you while you were following him. I got a question. Do you even know whose kid you're carrying? You could've told me up front that you were an ex of Ali's. I still don't remember meeting you but, who the fuck knows anything about anyone these days," Jabril said shrugging his shoulders.

"What all do you know?" I asked.

"A bunch of shit you never told me. I would've much rather heard about how you're working with Akeem's almost dead ass instead of how many surgeries you've gone through. You never needed a surgery from the pictures I've seen of you. I know for sure that you need a head doctor though. Something ain't right up there. The fucked-up part is that you were fucking with Carlos before Ali got killed. You might as well fucked his cousin too at the rate you're going."

I was scared because of how calm he was. Jabril was never the calm one, that was his brother Ish. To see him just standing here talking to me all normal and shit had me ready to break out and haul ass thru the graveyard.

"I don't know who the father is for sure. I don't think you have anything to worry about though,"

"It all makes sense now. I knew there had to be a reason besides love that you stayed around. Then I just thought that you didn't want to see me with Ciana. So, I never really thought about it much after that. So, what's the master plan? Do you even know the master plan?" He asked me.

"Akeem wants to kill you but, I think he really loves Ciana. Feelings were never part of the plan. I have some for you," I lied. I cared about him but, I cared about me more. There were times that I thought I loved him but, it wasn't anywhere near what I was describing to him or anyone else that he knew.

"Aht-Aht, wrong fucking answer. I ain't ask you about feelings or none of that other shit. I asked you if you knew the master plan. Fuck all y'all feelings. Don't try to change the subject either. The only thing that's keeping me from killing you and that bogus ass baby you're supposed to be carrying is the fact that there may be a chance that it's mine. Depending on how you answer that shit won't even matter anymore," he told me.

His voice was still calm but I know that he was getting fed up with my bullshit. I knew I was going to die sooner than later the cat was out of the bag. Even though he didn't have all the details but, with so many hands in the pot I doubt if anyone does know truly what's going on. There are so many agendas and ideas at play with this entire situation.

"Akeem wants to kill you for killing his brother and cousin, that's what I do know," I told him.

"I wasn't there that night. If one of y'all would've just come talk to me he would know that. We're past that point now. He's brought my girl and my daughter into this so all talking is out the window,"

"Your girl?" I asked.

"Focus, you know damn well what it is. Ciana ain't going no damn where, you on the other hand is getting ready to die. What's the deal with this Carlos nigga? I know you know the deal on him," he asked.

"He's a cop. He was the one that Ali was an informant for but, Akeem doesn't know about none of Ali's dealings with the cops. The only reason why I know is because they were talking about putting us in witness protection."

"Hold up in order for you to go with him; y'all had to be married. Were y'all married?"

"We were supposed to get married the weekend after that night of the meeting that you claim you didn't go to."

"Then you ended up fucking with his brother? Who the fuck haven't you fucked that I know? What was the purpose of all this? Akeem is a punk motherfucker for not approaching me like a man," he told me.

"You're not the easiest person to talk to."

"I'm not the easiest person to set up either," he said with a chuckle then he walked away.

I was shaking, nervous as hell because I thought I was going to die right here at Ali's grave. I watched his car pull off, as soon as he rounded the corner I hopped in the car. As I started the car I was looking around because for him to just walk off had me paranoid. I stopped at the light when I noticed a person sitting up in my back seat.

"Oh shit,"

I saw a flash then everything went dark.

CHAPTER 13

keem

I was calling Porsche's ass but, I guess she has her ass on her shoulders because she mad at me. She needs to understand that I need to use Ciana and her daughter as leverage to get Jabril off his game. I was on my way back to the house and her and I were gonna have a talk about her always running to the nigga. He may be her baby daddy but, she was my fucking girl. She had no business at that nigga's house or none of that shit that Porsche was talking about. I called her so she could have her ass at the house when I get there. I wasn't gonna be riding around looking for her ass either. I dialed Ciana again just to see where she is.

"What Akeem?" She answered with a fucking attitude.

"Yo, I don't know what the hell your problem is but, you need to fix that shit. I'm on my way to the house. I need you there when I get there because we have some shit to discuss."

"Yeah, okay."

"Leave that damn attitude in the fucking car. I ain't in the mood to be doing a bunch of arguing."

"You know what, I'm not trying to hear you talking to me all crazy and shit. You need to leave that tone you're using outside in the car or wherever you just left from. I think you've forgotten I ain't one of these yes bitches that you're used to fucking with. As long as you come correct then, there won't be an argument to have," she told me before ending the call in my ear.

I didn't want to but, I was gonna have to slap the shit out of her before all this shit was over. Her mouth was bad enough before but, now it's getting even worse. I didn't even think that shit was possible. Sometimes all you want is peace and quiet but, females these days didn't understand that shit. All Ciana had to do was be the girlfriend. It didn't take long after we first got together for me to realize she didn't know shit doubt Jabril's street shit. For a minute I didn't even think she knew he was in the streets at all. I should've known that he kept her at a distance for a reason. He was trying to protect her and the kid. Too bad this was going to be a death by association situation. Shit I probably could hurt him more if I kill her and let his ass live. There's no worse feeling than having the love of your life die because of some shit that had nothing to do with them.

I was pulling into the neighborhood that Ciana's house was located. I tried to call Porsche again of course her ass didn't answer. She was going to be the next one on the death list. It was always in the cards for her to die. It just so happens that I found something for her to do by getting close to Jabril. I didn't need her the way she thought I did. She was good for some on-call head and pussy. The fact that I knew she was dealing with my brother on a deep level showed me just how grimy she was. I also suspected she was dealing with someone else besides me and Jabril. I didn't have proof but, I know when shit ain't right. She was sneaky as fuck and for me to peep that shit made it even worse. I had secrets of my own so I didn't have the time to follow down behind her to find out what else she was hiding. The fact that I didn't care about her like she thought did help me see her ass for what she really was. Porsche was just trying to find a sucker to take care of her for the rest of her life. I still don't understand what my brother saw in her. I just knew that when I got inside her that I would be seeing Allah, Jesus, Jehovah, and all those other gods. Instead all I saw were the ugly ass sex faces she would make. Ciana's pussy was way better than Porsche's I know that for damn sure. I don't see how Jabril can keep fucking with her after being up in Ciana.

Parking my car alongside Ciana's truck I took a deep breath because I knew I was entering a war zone right now. I was hoping that she would have her attitude in check but, knowing her that shit was going to be on full display. I put my key in the doorknob and made my way into the house. There was music playing, the lights were dim as hell which made it dark. I looked around but she wasn't nowhere in sight.

"Ciana, I know you heard the door close. Where you at? What the hell you up to in here?" I called out.

Turning the corner to walk into the living room I saw there was a chair sitting in the middle of the room. I was confused until I paid attention to the song that was playing it was 'Dance For You' by Beyoncé. She still hasn't answered me.

"Have a seat Akeem. I know you want to talk but, I think for right now we should just celebrate you coming home in one piece," she said in a 'come get this pussy' tone of voice.

She was dressed in a pink outfit that looked like it still wasn't finished being made. It wasn't covering shit for real. Her ass, titties and pussy print were on full display. I know I should've stopped her from what she was doing so we could sit down and talk about her and her baby daddy but, my dick was on concrete right now. Maybe if we gave each other a nut then the conversation wouldn't be so damn hostile. I took a seat and waited on her next instruction. She started dancing around and showing me her ass and her pussy. I had to remember to ask her if she had ever been a stripper before her moves were on point like a motherfucker.

"Damn, you've been holding out on me. I need to go out of town more often," I said smiling.

"Close your eyes baby, I have a surprise for you," she whispered in my ear. Following her lead, I did as she asked. I could feel her tying up my legs and hands. This only made me even more anxious about the sex games we were going to play tonight. "Open them baby," she whispered then licked my earlobe.

I opened my eyes and to my surprise I was looking at Jabril's punk ass sitting in a chair directly in front of mine. He had two niggas on each side of him with guns pointing at me.

"What the fuck?" I said.

"Sup, I heard you were looking for me. Oh shit, my bad it was that you were looking to kill me," he said snapping his fingers like he had just remembered what he just said. "So, what the fuck is the problem?" He asked. I looked around for Ciana and she was nowhere to be found. His ass started laughing at me. "Oh, you're looking for Ciana. She's back there taking off that bullshit that she had on!" He yelled loud enough so she could hear him.

"Fuck you Ja. You said play the role and that's what the fuck I did. The next time you ask for my help I'm gonna tell your ass no straight like that," she argued as she came in the room with a sweat suit and some air force ones on.

"Now that's what the fuck you better had put on. You not gonna be satisfied until I choke the shit out of you. Then you rubbing ya pussy all on this nigga like you didn't know I was here. You better hope I don't shoot your ass too tonight. I told you to dress sexy not like a fucking thot," he told her.

"You didn't think I looked sexy. I bet Akeem thought I did. As a matter of fact, I know he did cuz I had him drooling, all ready to gobble up this pussy," she told him.

"I'm gonna fuck you so hard tonight that your damn eyes gonna be bleeding. I saw that licking shit you did too. Don't think you got away with that bullshit. I said make the nigga think he was gonna get some pussy. The key word in that sentence is think. Your ass went too damn far and you know it. Your big head ass always loves to fuck with me. I got your ass tonight though," he told her. Her crazy ass started shaking around and shit.

"Ohhhh I'm so fucking scared. Oh, nooooo don't fuck me until I cum. I'm so scared," she said rolling her eyes at him.

"I swear I'm gonna slap them damn eyes out of your head and go play craps with them if you keep rolling them shits," he told her.

Did these two motherfuckers forget that I was tied to a got damn chair looking at them?

"Stop trying to threaten me all the damn time. I did what you asked but, that ain't enough for your ass. You always gotta criticize some shit. I even caught my first body today and your black ass still hasn't told me thank you. You're a fucked-up individual," she argued.

What the fuck she means she caught her first body? What the hell is going on?

"My bad that was some sexy shit too. When you texted, me saying that shit was done I was proud as fuck of you. I said hell yeah my wife did that shit," he told her.

. . .

Wife? When the fuck did they get married?

"If you two want to argue you can let me the fuck up out of here. I know you don't have me here just to see y'all go back and forth," I said speaking up.

"Damn homie you big mad or little mad? Baby go head to the house and get ready for your dicking down tonight. You can be sleep if you want to. I'm not gonna wake your ass up I'm just gonna dive in that pussy," he told her then he gave her a kiss.

I couldn't help but watch her ass sway in those damn sweatpants. I know females go off about a guy being in ball shorts or sweatpants but, there was nothing like seeing a nice plump ass in some tight sweatpants.

CHAPTER 14

abril

I know this mother fucker ain't sitting here tied the fuck up, twenty minutes away from death checking out Ciana's ass in those sweatpants. I was going to bust his fucking head open but, he may as well have his last look at that beautiful ass that was mine and mine alone.

"That ass is something else ain't it?" I asked him as I adjusted my dick. "I can't wait to get in u tonight," I said shaking my head. Ciana knew she was gonna be knocked up real soon.

I turned back to Akeem and just looked at him.

"Okay so why the hell you got me here tied up and shit?"

"Oh, you're one of them niggas. How you gonna be running around telling mother fuckers you gonna kill me but now that I'm sitting in your face you don't know shit? You a punk ass bitch in real life like a mother fucker huh?" I told him.

"Fuck you!" Akeem yelled.

"Man cut the bullshit. Just tell me what the fuck is up."

"You got me here, acting like you know all the answers. Why the fuck you got me here if you already know what the play is?" He asked.

"I see why ya brother never mentioned your ass. You ain't nowhere near the man that he was. Come on man, we all here, get yo shit off ya chest. Now mind you I'm not gonna keep asking," I told him.

"I wanna know why you killed my brother and cousin," he finally said. Seeing him man up about his bullshit made me smile.

"See, that shit feels good as hell to let that shit out don't it? I don't know who told you whatever they told you but, I didn't kill Ali or y'all's punk ass cousin. True enough I was supposed to be there that night but, I got a call and had other shit to do," I told him looking him in the eye.

"Bullshit, he told me that he was meeting you. You took my brother from me," he yelled with tears in his eyes.

I hurt for him because Ali was my dude. Yes, I looked at his ass differently since finding out he was working with the cops but, there ain't shit I can do to change it. He knew the chance he was taking when he started working with them.

"Did you know he was a CI?" I asked Akeem.

He looked up at me like I had called his mom a trifling bitch. Just from that look alone I knew he had no idea. That only means that there was more that he didn't know as well.

"How the fuck you gonna lie on the dead? Just say what you did that night. You know you did it, just admit the shit," he said. I laughed at the way he was moving around in the chair like that was gonna help him get free.

"I know how you feel because I felt the same way when I found out about the shit. Sure, enough your brother, cousin and my friends were indeed working for them folks. Porsche knew about the shit too; she was saying they were gonna get married and shit. That's the only way they could both get placed in witness protection. There's still some questions that I have but, you can't answer those for me. Porsche can't either," I said laughing.

Every time I said her name I wanted to kill her ass over again. I should've known that there wasn't a loyal bone in her body. She's been under the knife so much that she was running out of shit she was born with. I meant to ask Ciana what color was the blood that came out when she shot her. I bet you that shit was clear as hell just like that botox shit and them jelly packs that they put in her titties and ass. I took my phone out to text her ass before I forgot to ask the question later.

> *Me - Bae what color was the stuffing when you broke the barbie doll.*
> *Her - what the hell are you talking about?*
> *Me - the plastic bitch that you threw out for me.*
> *Her - red why the hell you ask me that shit*
> *Me - I was thinking her shit wasn't red since she's a plastic bitch ya know*
> *Her - Where is Akeem?*
> *Me - Jus because of the situation I'm gonna answer you but let this be the last time you ask me the whereabouts of another nigga*
> *Her - so damn extra r u done yet*
> *Me - no my mind is all over the place.*
> *Her - focus and make it quick because my pussy is drying up*
> *Me - I don't care how dry it gets you better not touch it*
> *Her - go handle ya bizness and stop fucking with me*

"What type of shit are you on? You got me here to lie and say you didn't kill Ali, I had to suffer while you and shorty fussed like y'all were at the crib, now ya black ass is texting. What the fuck are you trying to do bore my ass to death?"

I looked at him and started laughing. I was laughing so hard that I had tears in my eyes. He was right but that shit was kind of funny talking about me boring him to death. Him looking at me like I was crazy made the shit even funnier to me.

"I didn't kill Ali. I have an idea of who did though," I said then I looked at my phone because it went off again.

"Nigga, what the fuck man? Who killed my brother and cousin if you didn't do it?"

"Ya boy Carlos, that's who did it."

He started laughing harder than I was. I gave one of the goons a head nod letting him know to bring me the folder. I opened the folder and shook my head as I went through the papers. I pulled out a picture of Carlos standing on the steps of the courthouse. He was talking on the phone but, you could see the gold shield on his belt. He had the whole cop vibe going on. It was plain as day. I admit if I hadn't seen the pictures I most likely wouldn't believe that dude was a cop. I admit he has some snake-like qualities but, I would never think cop just by looking at him.

"That's bullshit. That nigga ain't no cop he's done more shit than I have. Ain't no way I'm gonna believe that," he said. I knew that was coming so I placed another picture in his lap. It was a picture of Ali, Carlos and another guy talking in what appears to be a restaurant. That picture was followed by a few more. You could tell in a couple of them that Ali was uncomfortable being there. It seemed that he was forced or pressured to do whatever it was that he was doing. "My brother ain't a fucking cop; fuck all this bullshit you're talking. How you gonna slander the man's name like that?" he fussed.

"Says the nigga that's been goin around telling everybody I killed his fucking brother," I said.

My voice got a little elevated because I was fucking tired of telling this mother fucker I didn't kill his people. Fuck it if he wanted to think I killed him so the fuck what. I was tired and needed to be in some pussy that belonged to me right now. He really didn't want to believe that his brother was working with the cops for real. He could hold on to that shit all he wanted to the shit was true.

"Who was supposed to be there besides you? WHO THE FUCK KILLED MY BROTHER???" He yelled.

"I know who it wasn't. It wasn't the same nigga that killed you," I told him before placing a bullet right between his eyes. "Cut his fingers off leave him there and burn the house down," I told the fellas.

"Okay boss," they said.

"Y'all did get everything moved out of here like I told you to yesterday, right?"

"Yeah we put all the furniture and shit in the storage and took the paperwork to your house. We got you boss believe that," one of them said. I only gave a head nod in return.

"I thought you only did shit like that when someone stole from you," one of them said.

"Well, he did say he was going to kill me, ain't that stealing my life," they just looked at each other. I went out the door ready to get up in Ciana. I need a son soon.

CHAPTER 15

shmael

It had been years since I had to conduct an impromptu meeting of this nature. This couldn't wait until tomorrow. Shit, it couldn't wait for the fifteen minutes that it took for me to get to where the nigga was waiting for me. I was pissed to the point that I wasn't Ishmael the fine ass businessman that people were so used to seeing these days. I was Ish that street nigga that would body a nigga in a heartbeat. When I got the call I almost had a fucking heart attack. There were so many questions that I needed answered. My palms were sweating, head was pounding, and my fucking trigger finger was itching like a motherfucker. I pulled up to the building not caring about the no parking signs, I parked and got out of the car. I walked through the lobby. I'm sure my face is the reason why everyone stopped what they were doing to look at me with fear and apprehension on their faces. My dress shoes were hitting the cement floor so hard that the noise that was produced on impact was the only thing that could be heard. I walked into the office in the back to see the motherfucker sitting at the desk as if life was just fine. He looked up to see me coming at him and he tried to get up but he was too late. I hit him on the right side of his forehead with a closed fist. I'm sure he got a few licks in but, I was too pissed off to feel them right now. We were tussling, fighting, and fucking up this office. I didn't come here to fight but, I'm sure he was expecting me to fight him with what he had done.

"Motherfucker I should kill your ass for real. How the fuck you make a move like that but, didn't say shit to me or Jabril?"

I had him pinned down with his back on his desk. My hands were choking the shit out of him. I never thought I would enjoy this shit especially not trying to kill him of all people.

"If.. your...big... ass would ... let ... me; I'll tell you!"

I realized that he was right. I let his punk ass go. I can't believe this nigga had made a move like that.

"Why the fuck are you still alive Tennison?" I yelled.

I couldn't believe the man that I had looked up too all those years turned out to be the fucking snake. This nigga was a fucking legend in the hood. He's the man that taught me most of the shit I know about the streets and business. He was coughing to get himself together but, he had one damn time to move funny and I was going to kill his ass for sure this time.

"Ishmael, you need to let me explain everything to you. I called you because I know you're the levelheaded one. Jabril's ass would've shot me," he said with a chuckle. I stayed stoned face because this wasn't nothing to laugh about. I went through so much shit after he died it could've broken me down worse but, I had to get it together. I was dealing with anger, grief, and depression from the effects of hearing that he had died from cancer. Now here we are years later and he's standing in front of me.

"That night I was supposed to be killed was the night I entered the federal witness protection program. I had agreed to turn into an informant so they could snatch up my supplier. The only way I agreed to it was that the cops had to leave you alone. I knew you were still transitioning to go legit fully. I told them to leave you and your brother alone. You getting out and then getting caught up in street shit was the last thing you needed. I was old and tired anyway so why not let the government pay for all my shit. You have to know that I'm telling the truth. I would never sell you or your brother out. I did this for y'all. I'm so proud to know I made the right choice," he told me.

"You can sugar coat that shit all you want it was fucked up to do that shit and not give us a heads up!"

I still couldn't believe his old ass was standing here. Now I know exactly what bittersweet feels like. I was mad that he did the shit, happy he wasn't dead, and ready to knock the shit out of him again all at the same time.

"Why so you could look at me like you're doing now? Youngin' I never did it to hurt either of y'all. Shit, if that motherfucking Carlos wasn't trying to kill Jabril I would still be tucked away. The last thing I wanted to do was bring heat to y'all. Seems like I did all this for nothing," he said putting his head down.

"Carlos? Don't you mean Akeem? Akeem is the one trying to kill Jabril because he thinks Jabril killed Ali. Y'all are confusing the fuck out of me right now. What happen to the days when if a nigga had beef he came at you about the beef? These new motherfuckers want to play cloak and dagger out this mother fucker. Who is Carlos and what does he have to do with this?" I asked.

We both sat down. I could see this was going to be a long night. After talking to Big Ten my first stop is gonna be to talk to Jabril. He isn't gonna believe this shit.

"Carlos is the agent that I was working with. He's on an ATF task force. He was the one that took out my supplier. I found out that he's been undercover. The first time I heard it I thought of you and your brother. He wasn't on y'all though.

He wanted Ali's ass too. That's why I had to take him out. Ali would've taken y'all down with a quickness. He was already jealous of how tight I was with y'all. I knew as soon as Carlos tells him that he can sing to get away scot free y'all were gonna be on the top of the list,"

"How the hell did you come back to kill him? You were already dead when Ali got popped."

"No shit youngin'!"

"Well, Jabril is thinking that Akeem is behind all this shit. He's planning on taking him out thinking all this shit will be done by then."

"Nah, you gotta cut the head of the snake off. Carlos is the head."

I pulled out my phone to call my brother, he needed to know what was really going on. It couldn't wait until the morning either.

"Yooo," he answered.

"Aye, did you catch the rat?" I asked.

"Yeah, that shit is done. That trap fucked that rat all up. Why what's up?"

"We have another rat?"

"What the fuck you mean another one?"

"Some dude named Carlos."

"The one that was working for Akeem. He's a cop right?"

"Nah, he's not just a cop he's an ATF agent. He also wants you on a platter. Are you home?" I asked.

"Nah, I'm on my way there now."

"Okay we're on our way. We'll meet you there."

"Hold up, who the fuck is we?"

"You'll see when we get there," I told him ending the call. Big Ten followed me out of the door.

"I'm really proud of who you turned out to be. I always knew you had the potential to do something more than be the biggest kingpin."

I heard him but, I wasn't in the frame of mind to say much of anything to him right now.

"Somethings and people die too early so there's a hole that forms. The hole isn't just a simple hole though so just anything can't go in it to fill the hole. That's what you left in me and Jabril when you did ya little dying shit. A big fucking hole, it was like losing a dad because that's what you were to us. You coming back now all full of hope and aspirations to just go back to life how it was is your way of filling the hole you made with some bullshit. I don't care about your reasons or none of that other shit you coached yourself on before you got here. The point is you lied to us. Who knows if you would've said something we might've understood? Instead of being the man you called yourself teaching us to be you hauled ass. That shit ain't cool at all. The only reason I didn't kill your ass is because I still deal with the pain of losing your ass the first fucking time," I told him.

I was serious as hell with him. He played us all no matter how he dressed the shit up. I was waiting on him to say something bur he never did. I think that was the best decision his ass has ever made.

CHAPTER 16

iana

I was trying my best to relax but, my mind was all over the place. I can't believe Akeem was straight using my ass to get to Jabril. It's wild how even though Jabril and I couldn't get along for shit we made a whole child out here in these streets. We co-parented a lot better than other people. We even got a long better after Iyanna was born. The fact that we always understood that we may not work as a couple but, we can work together helped us get to the point we were at right now. Every time we talked about us or the relationship that never got off the ground we never ended up arguing. It's weird as hell because I can remember the night that we still haven't talked about to this day. I had come over to drop off something for Iyanna. She was around three years old then.

"Why you keep acting like you don't know a nigga? I know we ain't together and shit but, you straight acting like I'm a stranger. I'm your child's father. If we are gonna do this co-parenting thing the right way you can't be all stiff around me," Jabril told me.

"Ain't nobody acting stiff around you Jabril. You need to stop exaggerating shit. I know you and old girl just got together and I'm not trying to overstep," I told him.

"Overstep? Now that's the funniest shit I've heard all day. You could never overstep when it comes to me. I'm not gonna try my hand with you no matter how fucking tasty you're looking right now. Sit down, have a drink or two with me," he told me.

"She ain't here?"

"Sit your big head ass down, Ciana. Even if she was here that will never change how I act around you and you know it. If you want to keep shit one hundred she knows it too."

"Don't try to kick it with me like I'm special Jabril."

He gave me a slick ass look like he wanted to say something but, decided not to. Jabril knew that there was always some sexual tension between us no matter who was around. Up until that night I tried not to be in the house or even a room with him alone. I don't know what it was about us but we were definitely sexual soulmates if there was such a thing. It didn't matter that we were both with other people at the time. He drove my yoni crazy. I could see him and the thumping would start. He could give me a hug and my nipples would harden. It was, and still, is ridiculous how my body reacts to him. The bad part about it is that his ass knew it. Even though I knew the tension was there I sat down anyway. We talked and laughed so much that night that I was too drunk to try to make it home. He was too drunk to take me anywhere.

"I can call an Uber so I won't impose."

"I wish the fuck you would. You better take your ass in one of those rooms and go to sleep. I promise not to come in the room and drop my dick off in you. We all know how my shooters are around your punk ass eggs. It wouldn't bother me if you left here pregnant. I know you want to try to make shit work with that nigga. However, you're gonna be the only one carrying my babies. You too special to be a one-night stand or a piece of convenient pussy. I would never treat you like one," he said as he licked his lips.

"So, you and your girl are doing good?" I asked.

"That shit ain't cute, Ciana," was his response.

"Let me go check on Iyanna," I didn't wait for him to say anything. I got up and went to her room. I was standing in the door looking at my baby sleep with her body parts thrown all over the bed. I laughed at how funny it was that for her to be so little she slept wild as hell. The fact that he had her sleeping in a Queen size bed didn't help. I was lost in my thoughts when I smelt his cologne from behind me.

"You might not like it but, we made a beautiful, smart little girl," he whispered in my ear. He was way too close to me so I tried to move away from him. "Nah, just let me hold you for a few minutes man damn. You know I miss your ass," he said as he wrapped his arms around me.

I think the alcohol had gotten to me because I melted in his arms. There we were standing in our daughter's doorway. His arms wrapped around me in a definite possessive manner. I closed my eyes to enjoy the safe, comfortable feeling of being in his arms once again. I felt his lips on my shoulder, then on my neck, then his tongue in my ear. My mind was telling me to leave while my heart and body were telling me to enjoy the feelings that he was giving me right now.

Akeem could make me cum but that's where it stopped. The sex with him was detached and so impersonal that a lot of times I did it just because I was his girl. There wasn't any passion in what Akeem and I did. However, with Jabril, he could make tears come to my eyes just by eating my pussy and sucking my nipples. The way Jabril catered to my body was something I've never gotten used to. While he was kissing and touching on me his girl and my guy were the last things on our minds. There was no way that something that was clearly wrong felt so damn right. Jabril didn't have to tell me that he loved me because I could feel it from his touch.

"Damn it," I moaned.

I could hear him chuckle at my outburst. I was trying not to say anything because I knew he would see that as an incentive to keep going. Just like I knew he would, his hand started moving down to my pants that I had on. I moaned some more this time my mouth was closed. If I would let the words come out of my mouth I would've been asking why he was moving so slow. I allowed him to move at his own pace. When I felt him slide his finger between my folds I bit my lip.

"Do you remember when I used to play in my pussy all the time? It's fucking perfect for real. So soft, smooth, wet, and warm," he whispered. He knew that him talking to me was only taking me to another level. I loved that shit, especially from him. His voice went straight to my soul. I felt him slide his finger inside of me. "Please let me have you tonight Ciana. If you want me to get on my knees to beg I will. I just have to have you," he said. I was unable to say anything at that moment.

Seeing that I wasn't going to resist anything that he wanted to do to me tonight, he removed his hand from inside of my pants. His finger was pushed inside of my mouth which, I gladly accepted. He took my hand and led me to the bathroom which was right next door. He pulled my pants down, then lifted me onto the counter.

"Jabril, hold on!"

"You want me to beg right. That's what I'm about to do so let me handle mine," he told me with a smirk then he dropped to his knees. My mouth dropped open as he attacked my pussy with his mouth and fingers. My hands went instinctively to the back of his head to hold him in place. "Give it to me babygirl, give me that good-good that I've been craving since you left me," he said as he looked at me with his mouth, chin, and beard covered with my juices. He played with my clit but, expected me to answer him. He knew I was at his mercy just like I knew it. He stood to his feet, pulled his dick out and entered me raw and fast. When he got inside me he looked at me and smirked. It was sad that even with the sexual tension still in the air for the moment his ass still found a way to be cocky as fuck. "He ain't fucking you like the queen that you are. Ain't no way you should be this tight. I'm saying you're straight strangling my dick right now," He slid me down to meet his strokes and then he proceeded to fuck me as if our lives depended on it.

The thing that I didn't know that night was that we were always going to be connected. After that session we made love all night long all over the house. The surprising thing about it was that I didn't regret or even feel bad in the least little bit about what I had just done. I left his house before Iyanna got up the next morning. I got home to see that Akeem hadn't called or come by all night. Jabril sent a text after I got home saying thank you like he had just borrowed money from me. The reality of it all was that he took my heart that night. We never said a word about that night after that. No matter how many times I would have random flashbacks or urges to call him for some more. Jabril and I just vibed like that, there was a lot between us that didn't have to be said. It had been that way since that day he busted up in the clinic to stop me from having an abortion. Instead of running to him to get the love that we both deserved I did everything in my power to stop us from getting together. I had to laugh at the thought of me running from him but, not getting anywhere.

CHAPTER 17

abril

I rode around for a few before going to the house to look Ciana in her face. I had to give me some time to come down from what I had just done. I know the nigga deserved it but, the fact remains that she could front all she wanted to I know she had some type of feelings for his lame ass. I had to get my mind right just in case she was all sad and shit about him dying. The last thing I needed to do was to cuss her ass out for the shit. She had killed Porsche today but, Ciana isn't built for this shit. The only reason why she did it was because she felt like it was something that she had to do. *'I owe that bitch an ass whipping but, a shot to the head will do'* is what her violent ass told me.

I had always known about Ciana's violent side she was hell on wheels when she wanted to be. I remember when she was pregnant we were constantly beefing. She wanted to act like she wanted an abortion but, I think she just wanted to torture my ass. The funny part about it all is that I didn't care what she called herself doing. She could sit around and cuss my ass out because I wouldn't go home or I kept asking her how she felt. One day we were at her place looking at some stupid ass reality show and I asked her how she was feeling, somehow that one damn question turned into a full blown argument. She ended up throwing the remote control at my ass. I was walking around with a knot on my head for almost two weeks. So, I was very well acquainted with her violent tendencies. There were other times but that was the most memorable because instead of getting mad the shit was comical as fuck. Ciana always had been a ticking time bomb, she wasn't as bad as I was though.

I assumed when Iyanna started going to school they were gonna have us on speed dial if she turns out like her parents. She was doing good so far but, she was only in kindergarten so I was still waiting. She didn't have a sane parent maybe the crazy would skip a generation. When I got to the house none of the lights were on. Maybe, Ciana went to sleep. I didn't think she would but seeing the house dark gave me hope. I just needed some peace and quiet but, just when I was getting out of the car my brother pulled up behind me. Instead of him getting out he rolled the window down and stuck his head out.

"Yo nigga, get in the car we got some shit to take care of," he yelled out.

"Nigga, do you know what fucking time it is," I said as I got in the car. He didn't say anything, he just pulled off like the damn police were behind us. I could see it in his face that something was wrong. "What the fuck is going on? Why the hell are you flying? Is there someone dying that I don't know? Where the fuck are we going?" I asked just to not get a fucking word from him. We ended up at his condo. He just got out and walked to the damn door. I don't have time for extra shit tonight. I had to check on Ciana. I know catching your first body was a big thing. I had been texting her but, she never replied to any of the fucking messages. I shook my head because I should've drove my car instead. If I would've then I would be able to take my ass home and say fuck whatever Ish had going on at the moment. I took my ass in the house after him he was talking to someone that was standing in the kitchen. From the angle I was standing I couldn't see their face. Ish turned to look at me standing in the foyer.

"I need you not to go off Jabril. We don't need y'all in here fighting and shit. I'm only saying it because I had to two piece his ass a few times before I actually sat down and talked to him," Ish told me making me look at him sideways.

"Who the fuck is in the kitchen?" I asked as I walked towards Ish and the kitchen.

We weren't at the main house where Bali and my niece were so I wasn't listening to shit about not fighting. If he felt the need to tell me not to fight or go off then that's exactly what I was gonna do. I just couldn't think of who would be here that I wanted to fuck up. Then the person that was in the kitchen stepped closer to Ish. *WHAT THE FUCK !!!!!!*

"Aye, what type of bullshit shit you got going on in here?" I asked.

The nigga that was standing beside my brother looked like an older version of Big Ten. I'm not saying he looked like he was senior citizen home old but, older than when I last saw him. I just stood there looking at this guy. I kept wondering if Ten had a brother that we didn't know about, shit maybe a cousin or something. There ain't no fucking way Big Ten was standing next to my brother right now. This guy had to be a damn relative.

"Jabril," Ish started to say but, I cut his ass off.

"Nah, I know who you are let this mother fucker speak," I said as I walked over to him. The closer I got the more I realized that it was indeed Big Ten. This mother fucker had played us; he played us all. Who the fuck could do some shit like that? "If you wanted to be dead so fucking bad why the fuck are you here now?" I asked standing in his face.

"Jabril, I understand you're mad but, don't get shit twisted I'm still the same nigga. You need to back the fuck up," he told me.

"What the fuck ya dead ass gonna do to me? How could you do some shit like that? Did you come to the fucking funeral mother fucker? Huh? Did you like seeing how tore up everyone was behind your, non-dead ass? You selfish mother fucker!" I bellowed right before I stole off on his ass.

We were going at it. I didn't hear my brother say anything during the time me and the dead man were going at it. By the time we finished going at each other the kitchen, dining room, and the hallway that lead to the foyer were fucked up. Ish was sitting at the table with his phone in his hand. Once we were both still he looked over at where we were standing.

"Y'all done?" He asked.

"How the fuck can you be so damn calm right now Ishmael?" I asked.

"Simple, I beat his ass earlier. Sit-down we have some shit to discuss. Don't worry about Ciana and baby girl they're at the house with Bali,"

When he said that I knew there was more than just the ghost of thugs past popping up. I just couldn't figure out what it was. There's not much that can top a nigga coming back from the dead.

"What's going on?"

"Carlos is the one behind everything," Ish told me.

"Hold up nah, it was Akeem cuz, he thought I killed Ali," I said looking confused.

"Ali was an informant; Carlos is the officer that he was informing. Akeem didn't know about all that. Porsche knew because they were gonna get married and go into witness protections together. Then she started fucking Carlos," Big Ten said

"Carlos? She was fucking that nigga too? I saw the pictures

and shit but, I thought she was on some snitch shit like Ali and Akeem. So, the bitch was fucking me, Akeem, Ali, and Carlos man I would kill that bitch if her ass wasn't already dead. Who the fuck does shit like that?" I asked. After listening to this bullshit, I was past pissed. I wanted to fuck everybody up. First this big-headed motherfucker was faking his death and shit now the bitch Porsche was basically a train on two feet. This can't be life right now. This shit wasn't making sense to me. My fucking head was hurting. I could feel my phone vibrating in my pocket but, I knew already who it is.

"Are you good?" Big Ten asked me. I just looked at him and still ignored his ass. This nigga was gonna have to tread lightly with me. I was ready to go another round with his old ass just to get the frustration out.

"When are we killing the nigga? We need to throw in his kids, wife, side-bitch, outside kids, shit if the nigga gotta damn gay cousin we killing him too. I'm sick of this bullshit. I should've got my ass out of the streets when you did Ish. This guns and roses shit is for the birds.

"Jabril I want to explain what happen for me to do what I did," Big Ten told me.

"Did he explain the shit to you?" I asked Ish. Ish nodded his head up and down. "I see you're good with whatever reasons he gave you. If you weren't then he wouldn't be here. If Ish is good with it then, I don't need the details. Keep that shit to yaself but, the next time your black ass does some shit like this give a nigga like me a heads up. I'm about to take my ass home. I'll be over here tomorrow to figure out how we gonna play this shit. We can't wait around too long with them other two dead," I told them both as I stood and headed to the door.

The only thing I want right now is a shower, my bed, and my woman beside me. Just when I thought I could kick back to enjoy life with Ciana here comes more bullshit. A nigga can't win for losing lately.

CHAPTER 18

arlos

"How the fuck is it that you've been on this case for this long but, you have NOTHING? You've wasted enough of the department's time. Don't be surprised if you get a call from Internal affairs due to the untimely deaths of people connected to your case. Do you know anything about what happened to them?" My Captain asked.

"Captain, are you implying that I had something to do with their deaths? Why would I kill the two people that can help my case get made? That's a reach and you know that shit. But, to answer your stupid question, no. It's fucked up that after all the time I've put in with the department you are sitting here asking me all these questions and looking at me as if I'm the criminal. I thought we were all on the same team. Are you looking to lock me up as well?" I asked.

Captain Martini thought his ass was gonna make me the fall guy for this bullshit. His old white wrinkly ass was gonna be shocked as fuck when I stopped fighting my urge to jump across his desk and hit him so hard in the face that his unborn grandchildren will feel it. I've been working on cases surrounding Ishmael and Jabril for almost six years now. I started out just trying to find a way to connect Ishmael to illegal activity. He was making his mark in the city and his name was traveling up and down the east coast. To the average person they would just think that Ishmael was just another get out of the ghetto story. I knew way more than the average person though. I knew all about the shit that they used to do for Tennison aka Big Ten. I've never been an ass kisser of Ishmael. The problem that I had was that Ishmael was a lot smarter than I gave him the credit for. I had gone through every type of record there was trying to pin something on him. I kept coming up with a blank. Then I just so happened to run into Ali. Ali was more street than Ishmael and his brother put together but, he wasn't built for jail or prison though.

I first met him when he got pulled over for a traffic stop. He was brought in due to suspicion of being intoxicated. He was brought to the station and questioned. I just so happened to be there that night and I recognized him from all the research and surveillance photos I had of Ishmael. He was the one that told me the reason why I can't find shit on Ish was because he was out of the street. He also let me know that Jabril was still in. That was when the focus of my investigation changed.

"Carlos, I'm talking to you!" Captain Martini yelled.

I was so deep in my thoughts I haven't heard shit that he said. He was still out of pocket for hollering at my ass though.

"Who the fuck you yelling at? I know you're my boss and all that but, don't get fucked up," I told him.

"You even sound like one of those motherfuckers now. I hoped that you didn't lose yourself in this investigation. I don't even recognize you right now. This is so disappointing," he said shaking his head.

"I'm not trying to sit here and listen to this bullshit. For all I know I can walk out of here and die before I get home. Instead of trying to protect me you're looking at me all sideways and shit."

He stood to his feet, slamming his hands on the desk. He leaned over to look me in the eye.

"If I find out you're doing more than investigating I will hang your ass out to dry. The last thing this department needs is another fucking scandal. I hope you did things the right way. I'm telling you now if you didn't we're gonna nail your ass to the wall and leave you there. You're suspended until further notice. Leave your shield and gun, then get the fuck out of my office," he told me.

I gave him the shit that he asked for and walked the fuck out. I got in my damn car and headed to Jabril's house. I needed to see if I could rattle her cage enough for her to tell me what really went on at her house. I know she knew something but, I needed to feel her out to see how I could get the information out of her. I know who killed Akeem it didn't take a rocket scientist to figure that out especially when you know all the details that played a part in Akeem getting his ass knocked off. The problem was that I don't have the proof. Talking to her could help me find out if they knew about my involvement and the proof I need to lock Jabril up for killing Akeem.

Her house had been burned down and that was where Akeem's body was found. The coroner is saying that the body is too burned to tell if anything had killed him before the fire. I knew that she would be at her baby daddy's house being that she was temporarily homeless. It was a major hit for her to lose the house but, to find out Akeem was in there as well had to be a major blow for her to handle. Ciana was a strong woman she could survive through almost anything I'm sure.

At the moment I wasn't concerned about saving my already lost career. I could see it on the Captain's face that I was done as far as the department goes. When Ali died they were sympathetic about it. Now that there were two more bodies connected to me that were found last night no sympathy was being given at all. It doesn't matter how many years have passed in between; the fact of the matter was that people around me were dying before their time. I would be looking at me too if I was the Captain. While they were looking at me I was looking at someone else. I pulled up to the house that Ciana and Jabril shared just as she was getting out of the car. It was around one in the afternoon so I know that she knows that Akeem is dead by now. I have to find out if she was the one that killed them. If I can pin the murders on her that can save my ass.

"Ciana, hey hold up," I called out to her back that's at the front door.

"Carlos, what the fuck do you want?"

"Aye, hold on why you so damn hostile? I just found out about Akeem I was coming to check on you since you were his girl and all. I knew that you would most likely be here. I heard all about your house burning down. Shit is crazy out here. I'm sorry to hear that type of news. You don't deserve to be mixed up in anything that Akeem had going on."

"Why the hell would you check on me? You and Akeem were friends. You and I don't know each other very well. It's suspect as fuck that you're coming here all concerned and shit like we were buddy, buddy with each other. Why are you really here Carlos?"

She was looking at me as if I was the one that killed Akeem. That let me know that either she has no clue who killed him or she was a great fucking actor.

"I came to check on you that's all."

"I know you cared about Akeem but, if you cared as much as you say, you would've been there to stop whatever happened," she said with a tear coming down her face.

She was hurting right now. Maybe, I'm wrong for coming to

her like this. Maybe, I need to take a few days to myself just to figure out some things in my head. Nothing was making sense.

"I don't have all the details on what went down yet but, as soon as I get them I'll fill you in. Akeem had his flaws but, he didn't deserve to get killed. Let me know if you need anything for the service and shit like that. Keep me in the loop on the details," I told her before making my way back to the car. I pulled off with her standing on her porch looking at me. I needed to find out who killed Akeem because for some reason I think they are gonna come for me next. This investigation has been a problem since it first started.

CHAPTER 19

abril

"Jabril, Jabril where are you?" Ciana came in the house calling me like she didn't know I was in here sleeping. Before I could answer her she came busting up in the room.

"You're in here sleep and I'm getting questioned at the front door. Carlos just left here. He says he was checking on me since Akeem got killed last night and the house burned down. It felt more like he was trying to find out what I knew though."

I sat up in the bed thinking about what she had just said. If he was over here then he must be thinking that she's the one that killed Akeem. I got up to head to the bathroom and take care of my hygiene still thinking.

"How did he know you were here? Did he say anything about Porsche being missing?" I asked when I came back in the room.

"No, I was waiting on him to say something but, he never did. It was strange for him to even approach me like he did. I understand that they were friends and all but, it still seemed like something was off. He offered to help me with the funeral but, I never responded to that. How is it that he didn't say anything about Porsche or the fact that she was sleeping with Akeem as well? He didn't even mention her name. He might think I did both of them," she said as she sat on the bed.

"Did my baby ask about me this morning when you dropped her off?"

"Of course, she did. She told me to tell you that you need to be here when she gets out of school."

I was happy that Iyanna was going to a kindergarten that taught her so she will be ready when regular school starts. It's just crazy that they only go for a half of day. Iyanna was signed up for the afternoon session since she was hell to wake up in the morning. That's where Ciana was coming from when Carlos walked up on her. I know I needed to address this issue with Carlos sooner than later. He was indeed going to be a problem. Him being a cop was going to make the task a lot harder than it needed to be. I also needed to know what he was investigating in the first place. I've always flown under the radar. Why would he be hanging around now just when I'm trying to get out of this shit?

Ciana was worried about her being a suspect but, that was the least of my worries. If her name ever came up as a suspect I would confess to keep her out here. The last thing she needed was to be in prison. She needs to be here with Iyanna raising her to be the woman that she is destined to be.

"I'll be here but, I need to get Ish over here so we can talk. Let me go call him," I told her as I kissed her on the cheek and headed to the Diva Den that she had here in my damn house. I was tired as hell when I came in last night. I was happy that she was in my bed instead of in the room with Iyanna because I didn't want to sleep alone. There isn't a way for me to do that since that night I got back inside of her. If she wasn't next to me I wasn't going to be getting any sleep at all. She had taken over my world once again. I had to find a way to separate her name from Akeem's death.

"Hello," Ish answered.

"Yo, Carlos just left here talking to Ciana about Akeem's murder. He didn't come out and ask her did she do it or nothing like that but, I'm sure that was his reason for coming."

"I'm waiting on Pete to bring me the records of the investigation. We need to know what they were looking for and why. After all these years of being in the streets why were they looking at you now? I guess you could say that they were looking when Ali was an informant for them but, I have an idea of how your name got thrown in the pot. I know you said something about one last deal but, are you still gonna do that or what? I need to know so I can weigh our options before deciding on the next step,"

"Nah, I'm done I'm meeting with the fellas tonight to let them know. They can do what the fuck they want to do with the inventory that I have. I want to spend the rest of my days shooting up Ciana's club and spoiling my daughter. It would break my heart to have to talk to her through some damn penitentiary glass."

I had been thinking about that for a few days now. When it was just me, doing all this illegal shit was worth it. The adrenaline rush is addictive. After Iyanna was born the rush came from seeing her do shit like walk, say da-da, hold her own bottle, and shit like that. I suppose you can say that I'm growing up and looking at shit totally different. When Ciana came in the room to tell me about Carlos I had a feeling that I've never felt move thru my body. I was spooked about her getting into some legal shit behind this. I never want to feel that again.

"Yeah, I understand. You know I'll be right here with you to make sure all your shit gets done in the right way. There's no better feeling than going to the club and not have to worry some nigga trying to catch you slipping. You know you're always supposed to watch your surroundings but, it's different when you're legit."

"I here ya. Let me go in here and talk to Ciana some more. I think she's a little shaken up still."

"Cool, call me later Pete should have that info by the time you and Ciana finish fucking," he said with a laugh.

"Man, I said we were going to talk not fuck."

"Yeah, okay," Ish said then I ended the call.

Fucking is not on the agenda right now but, I'm sure we would end up that way before Iyanna gets out of school. I go to the room and Ciana was standing at the window just looking out of it. She looked worried but, I've seen her like this only one time before. That time was when I busted up in the abortion clinic to stop her from killing my baby.

"Is everything okay?" She asked but, didn't turn to face me.

"Yeah, everything is good. What's on your mind?"

"Life, just how we ended up here."

"Where exactly is here Ciana?"

"Us being back together making a go of the family thing. I never thought this day would come. We were so busy trying to prove each other wrong to give our relationship a fair try the first time. One night we were just fucking to scratch each other's itch and then it seemed like the next day we were parents and a family. I think it all just happened too quickly. This time we've had apart helped us in my opinion. It gave us time to get to know each other so that we are friends before anything," she told me.

For the first time this morning I noticed that her hair was up instead of down or in a ponytail. Her sexy ass neck was showing and calling my name. I heard loud and clear what she was saying but, my mind was in the gutter right now.

"You might be right. Other than us getting with people that we had no business being with and settling for them; I wouldn't change the road we traveled. I appreciate you more now than I did the first time around," I told her.

I can't say I told her that for her benefit because it was more for me. I needed her to understand where I was coming from just in case things went in the wrong direction. I had never had to go up against a cop before. The most dealings that I've had with them motherfuckers was them pulling me over for bullshit and reading their name on a list of the ones that owed Ish a favor or two. I know that we're a big deal. It was more of Ish being a big deal than me but, I was cool with that. I'm not the boardroom type of cat anyway. All that was up Ish's alley though. He loved that shit so that's why he was well-known. I guess I was known too if the fucking cops were investigating my ass. This was a new ball game for me. I needed her to know where I stood with her just in case I didn't come out of this shit breathing. I know if I said it like that she would get all upset and shit. I never understood why people didn't want to talk about death. It was coming to all of us eventually. Hopefully, mine wouldn't be coming soon.

CHAPTER 20

*B*ig Ten

I've been back for a few weeks and I was still nervous about what I was about to do. There wasn't much that shook me but, this meeting or should I say pop up has me shook beyond belief. I never wanted to end up here. I thought that when I left here I would never come back. Yet, here I am. I got out of the car and walked into the eatery. She had changed the place around and it looked damn good in here. I should've known that she was going to spruce the place up. Walking into the lobby area there was a picture of us that I had forgotten about. She was so excited that day and beautiful as ever.

"I'm so proud of you Stephanie," I told her as I held her in my arms.

She thought that I was holding her tighter because of the grand opening of her restaurant that she'd worked so hard for. I was holding on to her because this would be the last time that I would be able to do this. The plan was already in motion for me to disappear. I contemplated on telling her what was going on so many times that it was hard for me to focus on the joyous occasion at hand. As she walked around laughing and talking with everyone I stole a picture of her.

"I did it baby! Thank you so much for believing in me and my dream," she told me.

Her brown skin and brown eyes always mesmerized me. Her beautiful outside matched her beautiful soul. She was the most gracious and caring woman that I've had the pleasure of coming across. I'm sure if I were to stick around we would end up with at least five kids. I began to feel sick to my stomach thinking about all the pain that was about to come her way. I was a man so I made sure that she wouldn't have to worry about money or bills for the rest of her life. I know the money wasn't going to dull the pain but, this is how things had to be done.

"It's all good. You know I'll always love you and have your back even after I'm dead and gone. You just remember me that's all I ask," I told her.

"Why are you talking about death so much? I know what the doctor said about the cancer but, you have to have faith that everything is going to be okay," she told me.

"Yeah baby, I know," was all I could muster up to say.

The picture that was hanging in the entry way was from that day. One week after that the doctor that I paid made phone calls to her and Ishmael letting them know that the cancer that I was claiming to have had taken a turn for the worst. He also told them that I was scheduled to have surgery the next morning. They were all there from what he told me. Six hours after the fake surgery was to have started he went out to inform them that I had died from complications while in surgery. Looking at that picture brought tears to my eyes.

"How can I help you today sir? Will you be dining alone, today?" The cute little hostess asked.

"Is the owner here today?" I asked.

"Yes, would you like me to go get her for you?" She asked.

She had to be one of Stephanie's kids because she had her eyes and smile. I got so caught up in looking at her that I lost my train of thought.

"Sasha, it's time for you to take a br...," Stephanie started to say but stopped when she saw me. We just looked at each other.

"The years have been good to you, Stephanie," I told her.

I couldn't help but smile at how good she was looking. This is the woman that had my heart and soul wrapped up with her. The woman that I should've taken with me, instead of leaving her to grieve behind me. Out of nowhere she slapped me so hard that I know I had to have a handprint on my face.

"How could you do this shit to me?" She asked with tears in her eyes.

I put my head down because I was beginning to feel like shit standing here in front of her. Maybe, this wasn't a good idea for me to come here but, I couldn't be this close to her and not see her. I rubbed the part of my face that was stinging not only from the slap but, from the pain that was on her face and in her voice.

"If we could go somewhere and talk about everything. I had to come see you,"

"You want to talk to me? I go talk to you, or what I thought was you twice a week. I tell you about everything that's happened in life. I cry because my heart has been aching for you all these years. I stopped going to church after we buried whoever the fuck that was in that casket. I was mad at the world and the lord for taking you away when everything was just starting to look up for us. Tell me Tennison were you somewhere in the bushes laughing and looking at me cry to a headstone knowing your black ass wasn't the one in the dirt?" She fussed.

Now she had everyone looking at us. I ran my hand across my bald head trying to gather my thoughts. I knew she wasn't going to run to me with open arms but, to see her in so much pain was affecting me.

"Mama who is this?" The young lady asked.

There it was another pain shooting through my chest. I knew that Stephanie would move on eventually but, to see the child she made with another man took the little bit of hope that I had left. I looked between the both of them waiting to see how Stephanie was going to answer the question. When I left Stephanie didn't have any kids but, here this almost grown female is calling her mama. A lot of shit wasn't adding up and it wasn't just me coming back from the dead. Now I was getting more and more pissed at the fact that Stephanie hadn't answered the damn girl yet.

"How old are you?" I asked her since Stephanie still hadn't said shit.

"Fourteen," she answered.

My eyes went to Stephanie because she needed to start explaining what the hell was going on here.

"Stephanie, I know I've done some fucked up shit in my day. I never did any of it to you though. I need you to answer her and do it quick because I feel like I'm not the only one with mother fucking secrets," I barked.

"Call TJ and tell him to come up here," Stephanie said to Sasha.

"Man look I ain't got time to meet your new nigga. I was gone so I'm not tripping on none of that. I didn't come here to disrupt your life or no shit like that. I came because after all this time I still love you. I know I've done some fucked up things but, please tell me you didn't keep my child away from me," I said.

She was just standing there silently crying. She looked like she was about to pass out but, the way I'm feeling right now she could hit the floor and I would step right over her scandalous ass. She had me fucked all the way up as Ish would say. Sasha came back with a little boy that looked like he was about ten or eleven. You could look at both of them and tell that they were brother and sister.

"Tennison," she tried to talk to me to explain what the fuck I'm looking at right now.

"Nah, don't come at me with that Tennison bullshit, Stephanie," I said shaking my head.

"Oh cool, I never met anyone with the same name as me before. My name is Tennison too," the little boy said. My head turned in the direction of Stephanie so fast I know I had to look like the little girl on the exorcist.

"I need you to look me in the eye and tell me the fucking truth!" I yelled. I didn't care that people were looking at us. I didn't give a fuck about her crying or looking like she was going to pass out. I need her to say the shit to my damn face.

"Sasha and TJ this man, is your father," she said looking at me.

Tears rolled down my face. How the fuck did she hide two damn pregnancies from me. We were always together. I thought she loved me. Why hide my damn kids? What type of games is she playing with me right now?

"Everybody get the fuck up and get the fuck out," I said as I walked past Stephanie into the dining area of the restaurant. People were just sitting there looking at me. "I know y'all fucking heard me. Get the fuck out we're closed. Don't worry about paying for shit just fucking leave!" I yelled.

They finally got the hint that wasn't fucking around. I watched as they all got up gathering their things and rushing out of the door. Once the last person was gone I locked the front door, went to check if anyone was in the kitchen or the bathrooms before going to stand in front of Stephanie and my kids. *My kids.*

"Tennison you need to calm down. You're scaring them," Stephanie said.

"TJ do you play ball?" I asked.

"Play basketball, football, and baseball, sir," he answered.

"You can call me whatever you want besides sir. That sir shit is for niggas that's old like my pops and shit. Sasha are you into any activities at school?" I asked.

"I'm a majorette," she said with a big smile.

"Do y'all have phones?" I asked, they both pulled their phones out. I took them one by one and called my number so we could get in contact with each other.

"Tennison," Stephanie was trying to talk to me again. I shot her a look that made her shut her damn mouth. I could choke the fuck out her right now.

"Y'all go head and hang out. Me and your mother have a few things to talk about. I'll be back out right after. I looked at Stephanie, her eyes dropped to her feet. She started walking to her office with me hot on her heels. When we got in the office I took a seat because I was planning to stay all night so she could explain to me how I have two kids that I don't know about.

"Tennison, I'm sorry that I never told you. I got pregnant with Sasha a little bit after you got really big out in the street. Do you remember the night you got locked up? The night that you and John got caught up in some fight or whatever," I nodded my head letting her know that I understood what she was talking about. That was the first time I had gotten locked up since her and I made things official between us. I was more worried about her walking away than anything else. I got locked up for damn near five years behind that bullshit. *Wait a minute, hold the fuck up.*

"Are you sitting here telling me that you were carrying Sasha while I was locked up? If that's what you're gonna say then you're way out of line for that shit. Where the hell has she been all this time? Where was she all those years before I left? I have a bunch of questions and you're not giving me the answers!" I yelled.

"How can I when you're just coming up with your own answer before you even ask me the questions? She was in Florida with my Aunt Janice,"

"When did she come back? Why didn't I know about TJ?" I asked.

"I found out I was pregnant with TJ a month after that fake ass funeral," she said rolling her eyes. "I went to the grave and told you that you were going to be a father. I even told you about Sasha," She broke down crying again. "Why did you do it? Why did you leave like that?"

"I left so no one close to me would die because of my choices. I know that you always wanted me to get out of the streets. I was in so deep that I couldn't see a way out. Then the cops started fucking with me. Dying was the only way I could walk away. I know you probably hate me for it but, if the same situation comes I would do it again in a heartbeat. Don't try to kill me or beat me up I already had to fight Ish and Jabril," I told her.

"Oh yeah," she said.

"Don't even think about it. Look I know we have to do a lot of talking and getting to know each other again. I'm not going to try to bulldoze my way into your lives. I just want to get to know my kids," I told her.

"We can do that. We just need to take it slow," she told me.

I felt a little better but, how was I going to be a father to two kids that thought I was dead.

CHAPTER 21

abril

I looked at the dirt and shit ready to get out of this dirty ass country. I don't understand how Cancun can be a part of Mexico. That was the best part if you ask me. Unfortunately, I wasn't in Cancun or none of the tourist spots. I was in the real and dirty part of Mexico. It was outside of Mexico City but, it still looked like I was moving back in time the further we got from the city. I came here to meet with Sheik to let him know to his face that I was done with all this illegal shit. It wasn't a lot of it that I was dealing with but, it was enough to start a whole investigation so that was too much. I never thought that me doing this would come to an end but, the shit going on around me was forcing the fuck out of my hand. We pulled up to this big ass house in the middle of the fucking desert. There was no fucking way I would be stepping foot back in Mexico after this.

"Mr. Lawson, Mr. Sheik is ready for you. What would you like to drink?" The maid asked.

"Nothing I don't plan on being here long," I told her.

Sheik was a man of money. He was born a prince of one of the places in Afghanistan. His family had stakes in most of the country's oil along with the illegal shit that he ran. You can't forget that his fucking pops is a king. I didn't mind dealing with Sheik because he was straight and to the point. He would tell anyone that he did the illegal shit because fucking pussy got boring. This wasn't a way of survival for him like it once had been for me. It was a form of entertainment.

"Ahhh Jabril my friend, it's wonderful to see you in good spirits and health. How is your brother?" He asked as we shook hands followed by us taking our seats.

"He's chilling making babies and shit."

"I already know what the reason is for this meeting. My only question to you is are you sure this is the move you want to make?"

"Yeah, I have a child that I want to see grow up. I can't do that peacefully if I'm still working with you."

"Ah your child, what about her mother?" He asked looking at me attentively.

"She's around," I said with a chuckle.

"I admire you for making the decision that you've made. I know I will never have that choice presented to me to make. In my country you can have multiple wives and even more children. The fact that I'm the prince doesn't hurt but, it's the same for all men as long as he can provide for all of his wives. The man is the head and all decisions that are to be made are made by the man and that is not up for debate. I can call the two wives I have upstairs down here for them to do all type of sexual things to you and they would hop to it. So, you see there is no reason for me to take into account their feelings in my decisions because their wants are the same as mine," he said.

"Damn, so you run shit like that huh?"

"Yes, in my country the woman is nothing more than an ornament or a toy for a man's pleasure. In the United States your women have thoughts of their own. I know your woman wouldn't hesitate to walk away from you for putting your little family in danger. Instead of waiting for the drama that comes with staying in your choosing to get out for the betterment of your family. That is truly admirable."

I didn't understand if he was complimenting me or calling me a punk but, I left it alone.

"I'm relieved that you understand. I'm sure me pulling out will not hinder business at all. I've been scaling shipments back for the past year and a half."

"True enough you have. I knew this day was coming. I wish you the best and would like an invitation to the wedding that I'm sure is in the works."

"How are you so sure?"

"If a woman makes you change up shit you've been doing all of your adult life you better marry her," he said with a laugh.

I laughed with him but, I agreed wholeheartedly. Ciana was the one that matched and challenged me at the same time. She was everything that I wanted and was scared of. I didn't stay around to shoot the shit with Sheik due to the fact that I had to get back home. I had a party planned for my baby tonight that she didn't know about. It wasn't her birthday or an anniversary of any sort. This party was to celebrate the new beginning that we were about to embark on as a family unit. The ride back to the airstrip was filled with her texting me trying to figure out why I sent her a gown and shoes for her to wear tonight. It didn't matter how many times I told her that I wasn't going to tell, she still asked. Ish's nanny was going to keep Iyanna tonight with their kids. I laid back anxiously waiting for these three hours to go by. That was the beauty of traveling on a chartered plane. There weren't any stops to change flights or none of that extra shit. It was just the right amount of time that I needed to take a nap.

"Welcome back Mr. Lawson," my driver said as I entered the car awaiting my arrival on the tarmac.

"Is everything set?" I asked.

"Yes, sir, the Mrs. is a little upset by the lack of information that we were able to share with her. Other than that, everything is a go for the night," he told me.

I nodded my head nervous as fuck about what was about to go down. If tonight didn't clarify how I felt about her to her then nothing will. I called Ish while I was on my way to the place for me to get dressed.

"Is it done?" He answered.

"Yup I'm one hundred percent done and free."

"Well, you might be done but, free ain't what you are. I can't wait until you shut Ciana's angry ass up tonight. She's ready to fight all of us because we won't tell her anything. She called Bali a traitor and went off on me. It took all I had in me not to laugh in her face. Man, please come put this woman out of her misery. She's real hot about the fact that she's riding with us. I'll be glad when this night is over. You owe me and the wife a vacation where you keep all offspring born at that time," Ish told me.

"I got you and yeah I'm gonna have her ass speechless. I'll be there after I get dressed make sure she doesn't drink too much," I told him before ending the call.

I looked down at the ringing phone to see Ciana was calling my black ass again. I sent her to voicemail like I did all the other times. She was now sending text messages that I wasn't even going to look at. We pulled up at the house that I was changing my clothes in for the night. For once in a long time I was excited as hell to get to the club.

OOOOO

"You need to find you somebody safe to play with Jabril Lawson. How can you send me all this stuff today talking about we're going on a date just to have me being the third wheel tonight? I don't know what you got up your sleeve but, if you don't show up tonight you're gonna be sleeping on the couch for so long that you might end up moving all your shit into the living room. I can't believe you right now and you're not answering the phone. This just doesn't make sense," Ciana yelled into my voicemail.

I knew she was going to be fussing but, she was ready to fight my ass. I listened to the message on my way to the club. After hearing that I ended up deleting the text messages without reading them because I know they were a lot worse. The closer the car got to the club I started to get nervous as fuck. This was a major move for me. I hope she doesn't punch my ass in the face in front of everyone though. Stepping out of the car I smiled because I was stepping into my future. I gave the guy at the door the head nod and all the lights in the club were shut off.

CHAPTER 22

iana

I slammed the phone down after calling Jabril once again.

"I don't understand why you can't tell me what time he's going to be here. Nobody will tell me anything else but, if I were to get up and walk out of here then I'm going to be the one in the wrong," I fussed at Bali and Ish.

They both weren't paying me any mind. My anxiety was through the roof and no one was helping me by telling me what was really going on. I got up this morning to a note on Jabril's pillow telling me that he had some business to handle but, he would be back soon. Around lunch time a gift was delivered for me. It wasn't anyone's birthday or any anniversary so I was confused as hell. When I opened it there was a dark green gown, with matching accessories and shoes in the box. There was also another note from Jabril telling me that he was taking me on a date tonight. I started calling him after the first note just to hear his voice. Now after the second box I was calling him to find out what he had planned for the night. I asked everyone in the house but, no one had any answers. When I called Bali and Ish to find out what they knew they were playing dumb just like everyone else. By the time I got dressed I was irritated beyond belief. I had texted and called him all day he didn't answer not one of them.

"Calm down, he'll be here sooner than you think. Just relax have a drink," Bali said smiling.

She knows damn well I can't drink anything that will help my nerves. That's another reason why I was upset. He had knocked my ass up again. This time I know he did the shit on purpose. I've known for a few days but, with everything just now getting back to somewhat normal I was planning to tell him this weekend. I guess I can tell him tonight if he doesn't come here on some bullshit that will make me cut his ass.

The lights shut off out of nowhere. I sat up in my seat looking around in the dark just to see more darkness. The people in the club were whooping and hollering random shit out.

"What the hell is going on?" I asked.

"Come stand over here with us," Bali said.

I stood up looking over the balcony into more darkness. The grumbling of the crowd stopped when a bright ass spotlight was turned on at the front door.

"What the hell?" I asked.

I looked at Jabril walking in, dressed in a green suit. He was matching my dress even down to the color of the shoes he had on. My baby was looking some kind of fine. I forgot about being mad at him just that quick.

"I need to talk to y'all for a minute. You see I wanted to bring everybody here tonight because there's someone here that doesn't fully understand just how special she is. She thinks every compliment comes with a smart remark after it. When it doesn't, well, not for me. She has the most beautiful smile that can light up a dark ass tunnel. After you get past the hostility, feistiness, the left and right jabs you'll fall in love with her dry sense of humor or her corny ass laugh," he said as he walked up the steps to get to where we were. Bali was crying because that's what she does. I wonder how she held it together this long, if she knew all this was going to go on.

"Oh, wow this is; oh my goodness," I said shaking.

"Somebody's showing out tonight huh, lil sis," Ish said as he bumped me with his shoulder. I could only smile at him until Jabril got closer to me.

"Ciana, the best thing that ever happened to me was the night I knocked you up. The lord was on my side when we hooked up. There's no way any one can tell me that love can't come from arguments and cuss words. I never expected for us to end up here standing here matching looking fly and shit," he said smiling all hard sticking his tongue out. The crowd started clapping and making all kinds of noises.

"I love you Jabril thank you for doing all this for me!" I screamed. He took my face in his hands and gave me the most sensuous kiss that I've experienced so far in life. The thing that surprised me the most is the fact that he dropped down to one knee.

"So, baby mama you wanna upgrade and change your last name?" He asked as he opened up a box that held a ring that was absolutely gorgeous. I don't know how many carats the diamond was but, I do know that the reflection that it was giving off from the light was blinding.

"Yes! Jabril yes!!" I yelled at the top of my lungs.

He slid the ring on my finger then stood up to kiss me.

"That's how you shut shit down dawg!" Ish yelled as they gave each other a hug.

"Yess bihh!" Bali screamed as she looked at my ring. "Oh, best friend he did that with the ring. I was nervous because you know Jabril acts like he rode the short bus all the time. He did good though with this one. I damn sure didn't help him pick it out," she said cutting her eyes at Jabril.

"Man, you damn right you didn't. Everybody knows you don't know how to keep a damn secret. You would've helped me pick out the ring and sending Ciana pictures the whole time. I had to keep all this a secret to see the look she had on her face. I know you were pissed earlier baby but, do you forgive me now?" Jabril asked.

"Of course baby," I replied giving him a kiss.

"Congratulations to the lovely couple," an older guy said.

I had never seen him before. It was a weird vibe in the air when he made himself known.

"Just leave it alone for now. I'm sure Jabril will fill you in later or tomorrow," Bali whispered in my ear.

I know she could tell by the look on my face that I was confused as to who the hell this old guy was. I paid attention to everything so I quickly picked up on the fact that Ish was doing most of the talking with the guy while Jabril only took sips of his drink when the guy asked a question. I know he was using the drink as a way to avoid talking to this man but, the question I had was why.

"I have to go to the bathroom. I'll be right back," I said.

"I'm coming with you," Bali volunteered and looped my arm in hers.

When we got into the bathroom Bali checked the stalls to make sure we were alone. I looked at her like she had lost her mind because she was being extra as hell right now; even for her.

"The old guy is Big Ten," Bali said excitedly.

"I thought he was dead."

"Yeah, everybody did but, that's him in the flesh. I don't know all the facts yet. Ish always gets all weird on me when Big Ten is mentioned. I know whatever it was that made him fake his death had to be something major. You know how they would always talk about how Big Ten treated them like they were his kids and shit. Whatever it is had to be some life or death shit," Bali told me as she messed with her hair in the mirror.

"So, you're telling me that man is the person they always say is the one that taught them everything they know? That died a long time ago. You can't drop anything like that on me then act like it's normal. Then on top of all that you don't have all the details," I told her.

Bali wasn't on her job with getting information out of Ish. The only time she didn't find out the details is when he was holding out for whatever reason. I need both of them to get their mess together. I want to know what the deal is with old men coming back from the dead.

CHAPTER 23

ig Ten

I know that coming here tonight would be a gamble but, I had to talk to Ish and Jabril about a lot of shit. There was no way I was going to be able to sleep without letting them know what was going on with me and the decision that I made.

"What brought you out tonight? I know you never like coming to clubs and shit like that, what gives?" Ish asked while Jabril just gave me the death stare.

"Is there somewhere that we can talk just the three of us?" I asked.

"What for you plan on dying again? Just so you know we're not paying for no more funerals for your ass. The next time we just gonna pour some liquor out for your ass and keep it moving," Jabril said.

"You're gonna keep testing me and I'm gonna school your ass," I told Jabril.

I was tired of his bullshit. Don't get shit twisted I may be up in age but, I can break these young niggas down like it ain't nothing.

"We can use the office upstairs. Is everything cool though?" Ish asked and I follow them out of the VIP area.

"I can't answer that," I told him honestly.

When we got into the office Ish took a seat at the desk. Jabril stood by the door. I knew it was gonna take some time for him to warm back up to me but, he was getting beside himself. I was done taking his slick ass remarks and him looking at me like he can beat my ass. He had me fucked up.

"We listening," Ish said.

"I'm gonna handle Carlos so y'all don't need to worry about that shit with him," Jabril chuckled and that was the last fucking straw. "Do you have some shit you need to get off ya chest?" I asked.

"You came in here to tell us you're gonna handle Carlos for what reason exactly? I'm just asking so the motherfuckers in the back can understand where you coming from. I know you didn't think we were gonna congratulate you on stepping up. Truth be told your bogus ass moves started all this shit. You should be the mother fucker to fix it. So yeah you're funny as fuck to me right now," he said.

"This shit ain't on me. The whole point of me taking off was to get y'all out of harm's way," I explained.

"Exactly how did that plan work out? It worked out so damn good that you brought your dead ass back here to fix the shit you started. It doesn't matter what your intentions were the shit didn't stop when you left. You went and died for no fucking reason bruh. You think because you only snitched on who the fuck you snitched on made you the world's best snitch or something. Well, it didn't. When you left they did what they always do GO! FIND! ANOTHER! ONE! Get the fuck out of here with that I was helping y'all bullshit. You were helping you. The fact that you felt cornered by his ass to tell on us but, you didn't want to do it. You chose to run. Ain't shit heroic about running Tennison. Now if you would've stood ten toes down and ate them years they were holding over your head and still not snitch that right there is some shit I can respect. I don't talk when you're around because I have no words for your weak snitch ass," he told me.

I stood there taking in everything that he was saying. I couldn't say much in response to him because he was right. I should've handled it differently but, back then what I did made perfect sense. He left out of the office slamming the door behind him. I was literally speechless.

"You do realize that he's hurting behind you coming back. Jabril ain't good with feelings and shit. Neither one of us are but he's worse off than I am. You were the closest thing we had to a father or even an uncle. After you died man we both were lost for a long time until we learned how to lean on each other. Just when we start understanding and not dwelling on shit here you come all alive and shit. It's a lot to handle. I'm not gonna hold the shit against you because we all have our crosses to bare when we do die. You can thank my wife for changing my mindset. Just so you know I agree with my brother I just take my anger out on my wife's pussy every chance I get. He might come around but, then again he might not," Ish said shrugging.

"That's the least of my worries," I said shaking my head.

"What the fuck you got going on?"

"I just found out I have two kids that I never knew about."

"Get the fuck out of here. Who are the kid's mama?"

"Stephanie."

"No shit, when the fuck was she pregnant? I don't remember her being pregnant. I haven't been by there to check on her like I usually do but, when the hell was she pregnant?" Ish asked again.

"That's the bullshit part of life. When I got locked up that first time for five years she gave birth to my daughter. She claims she was pregnant with my son but didn't find out until after the funeral. I should've known when I saw the lil girl in the restaurant. Shit just don't make no sense. If she would've told me about my daughter it could've changed the way I was moving out here in the streets. A bunch of shit could've been done different. Stephanie said she didn't want the kids here and connected to me with all the shit I was doing. The shit still doesn't sit right with me. How can you sit there live with a man, sleep beside him every night, make plans for the future with him and not say oh yeah we have a kid? I just don't understand it," I said.

"What did she say about you being alive?"

"She slapped the shit out of me. I can still feel where her hand connected to my face."

Nothing was making sense it didn't matter how much I said it out loud either. This shit with Stephanie wasn't feeling right. I didn't want to think that she would do me dirty but, there was no other reason I could come up with. Even though the shit could've happened it just didn't feel right. She didn't look like she was telling the truth. The shit she was saying sounded rehearsed as it played back in my head. There was something else going on, I just didn't know what.

"Was you expecting her to hug yo ass? Man, you tripping thinking life is just going to go on like nothing ever happened. You gonna have to get used to the anger because every time you pop up on somebody that's what you're gonna get hit with."

"Yeah, I'm gonna get out of here. Like I said I'll take care of y'all's problem," I told him. We shook hands and I left to go talk to Stephanie because I still have questions. I needed answers my mind wasn't going to rest until I got them.

The ride to the restaurant was a quiet one. The radio was off and I was smoking a blunt. I just needed to think about some shit. The words of Jabril were in my head and the ones of Ish. Before I decided to come home I should've known this shit wasn't gonna be easy. It was hard as fuck. The more I thought about the things that Jabril said tears started to flow. I had royally fucked everything up. If I would've stayed and faced my shit there would be a lot of things that would be different. I pulled up to the restaurant it was a little bit after two in the morning. I figured she would still be here cleaning and shit but, something felt off. I pulled my car around back in the alley just in case some shit went down. The back door was open and I could hear voices. One of them was Stephanie and I could tell she was pissed and crying.

"Your ass told me you were handling it. Why the fuck is he back? How is he back roaming free?"

"Calm down I'll handle it. He's the last person that can connect the dots. Well, him and you of course but, we all know you're not gonna tell anybody," the man said. I knew that voice but, instead of making myself known I decided to keep listening.

"I haven't said anything after all this time. Why would you even throw my name in this shit?"

"You were the one that put me on Big Ten trail in the first place. I wonder how he would feel if he knew that you were my little spy with benefits back then. I can't believe you have him thinking my kids are his."

"What the fuck was I supposed to say? Your ass didn't call me to say he was back in town. I had to come up with something. Telling him they were his was the first thing that came to mind.

If you would've did what you were supposed to do this shit could've been done a long time ago!"

"Says the bitch that was fucking two niggas, married one and still acted single all for the sake of some info. I should've understood your position in life when he left everything to those two mother fucking brothers instead of your ass," Carlos argued with her.

"I only did it because if he would've left the money and shit to me you could've quit and we could've left town permanently. I just don't know why you kept fucking with the brothers after the fact. Even if you could bring them down it wasn't gonna get you any more money. If you would've left them the fuck alone he wouldn't have come back. Why can't you understand that?" She argued.

"Because he's just like you a greedy, lazy mother fucker," I said stepping inside of the kitchen.

They both looked like they had seen a ghost. I guess that's what I was to them.

"Tennison, umm, I heard you were back," Carlos said.

"It was only about the money huh?" I asked Stephanie. "Nah, don't forget how to talk now. You was just telling him how all this was his fault. How dare you come at the boys like that. You knew better than they did how much they meant to me. Why would you think I was going to leave you anything? You were set up to take care of yourself. I loved you but, you were never my wife so you should've known what the fuck it was gonna be. I deposited forty thousand in your account before I left because I knew you weren't gonna get shit from the will. You wanted more though huh?"

"Forty thousand? You never told me that Stephanie! Where's the money bitch?"

"I guess your police ass didn't figure that part of the puzzle out," I told him as I took my gun out. "So, y'all are married for real?" I asked.

They both nodded their heads up and down.

"What about our kids?" Stephanie asked.

"They'll be straight," I said.

I shot them both in the head. I stood there for a minute to decide what my next move would be. Shaking my head, I got in my car and drove off.

EPILOGUE

abril

I was happy as hell that the drama from a year ago was gone. After me getting shit off my chest with Big Ten he kept his word and then dipped. I know he still called Ish every now and then but, he stayed away from my ass. That was his best bet. I just didn't get how he brought us up telling us that loyalty is what matters the most. Come to find out when shit gets thick his loyalty wasn't to anyone but, his damn self. That shit bothered the fuck out of me. I honestly thought about killing his ass while he was here walking around like shit was sweet.

Ciana and I were married six months ago in a nice small ceremony. I was over the bullshit of putting on a big wedding for a bunch of mother fuckers that didn't give a shit about either of us. For our honeymoon we went to Tahiti with Ish and his family. We could've done the only 'us' type of shit but, we both didn't want to leave Iyanna with anyone. Somehow it turned into our little family going to Ish and his coming as well. It was lit as fuck though. The nanny came so it was cool as fuck to spend time with the family and be able to get fucked up and fuck the shit out of my wife at night. It was the best vacation I've ever had!

Ciana

It's crazy how you try to fight what is destined to happen anyway. I don't know if Jabril and I refusing to address the feelings we clearly had for one another contributed to all the foolishness that we went through. I know it was a factor. It hurt my heart to see him go through the pain of realizing that Big Ten was just as flawed of any of us out here. I know most of his life he would ask himself what would Big Ten do in many situations. Yes, he was pissed about what the reason was behind Big Ten faking his death but, he was extremely hurt as well. Ish knew that's why he never pushed him by talking about the Big Ten situation. They both handled it the best way they knew how. I know that Ish still talks to him from time to time but, that was Ish's personality.

I was now very pregnant and Mrs. Jabril Lawson. Some may say the time we were co-parenting was time wasted but, I beg to differ. That time taught us both that life is too short not to be happy. Although change is sometimes scary and all the time unpredictable you should never run from it. That happiness that you're trying to avoid can be the happiness that you are destined to have. All in all, it taught Jabril and I both to always go for happiness. It doesn't matter if you're scared or just don't understand what you're feeling still go for it. The journey of getting to know each other is just as important as acknowledging the feelings when they occur. No matter what you do in life always remember the worst thing you could ever do when it comes to matters of the heart is settling.

The End

Made in the USA
Columbia, SC
10 May 2024

35506384R00083